IT'S LIKE THIS, CAT

CAT

Emily Cheney Neville

 HarperTrophy®
A Division of HarperCollins*Publishers*

To
Midnight,
"Mayor" of Gramercy Park
1954–1962

IT'S LIKE THIS, CAT
Copyright © 1963 by Emily Neville
Copyright renewed 1991 by Emily Cheney Neville

CONTENTS

1
CAT AND KATE

My father is always talking about how a dog can be very educational for a boy. This is one reason I got a cat.

My father talks a lot anyway. Maybe being a lawyer he gets in the habit. Also, he's a small guy with very little gray curly hair, so maybe he thinks he's got to roar a lot to make up for not being a big hairy tough guy. Mom is thin and quiet, and when anything upsets her, she gets asthma. In the apartment—we live right in the middle of New York City—we don't have any heavy drapes or rugs, and Mom never fries any food because the doctors figure dust and smoke make her asthma worse. I don't think it's dust; I think it's Pop's roaring.

The big hassle that led to me getting Cat came when I earned some extra money baby-sitting for a little boy around the corner on Gramercy Park. I spent the money on a Belafonte record. This record has one piece about a father telling his son about the birds and the bees. I think it's funny. Pop blows his stack.

"You're not going to play that stuff in this house!" he roars. "Why aren't you outdoors, anyway? Baby-sitting! Baby-talk records! When I was your age, I made money on a newspaper-delivery route, and my dog Jeff and I used to go ten miles chasing rabbits on a good Saturday."

"Pop," I say patiently, "there are no rabbits out on Third Avenue. Honest, there aren't."

"Don't get fresh!" Pop jerks the plug out of the record player so hard the needle skips, which probably wrecks my record. So I get mad and start yelling too. Between rounds we both hear Mom in the kitchen starting to wheeze.

Pop hisses, "Now, see—you've gone and upset your mother!"

2

I slam the record player shut, grab a stick and ball, and run down the three flights of stairs to the street.

This isn't the first time Pop and I have played this scene, and there gets to be a pattern: When I slam out of our house mad, I go along over to my Aunt Kate's. She's not really my aunt. The kids around here call her Crazy Kate the Cat Woman because she walks along the street in funny old clothes and sneakers talking to herself, and she sometimes has half a dozen or more stray cats living with her. I guess she does sound a little looney, but it's just because she does things her own way, and she doesn't give a hoot what people think. She's sane, all right. In fact she makes a lot better sense than my pop.

It was three or four years ago, when I was a little kid, and I came tearing down our stairs crying mad after some fight with Pop, that I first met Kate. I plunged out of our door and into the street without looking. At the same moment I heard brakes scream and felt someone yank me back by the scruff of my neck. I got dropped in a heap on the sidewalk.

I looked up, and there was a shiny black car with M.D. plates and Kate waving her umbrella at the driver and shouting: "Listen, Dr. Big Shot, whose life are you saving? Can't you even watch out for a sniveling little kid crossing the street?"

The doctor looked pretty sheepish, and so did I. A few people on the sidewalk stopped to watch and snicker at us. Our janitor Butch was there, shaking his finger at me. Kate nodded to him and told him she was taking me home to mop me up.

"Yes ma'am," said Butch. He says "Yes ma'am" to all ladies.

Kate dragged me along by the hand to her apartment. She didn't say anything when we got there, just dumped me in a chair with a couple of kittens. Then she got me a cup of tea and a bowl of cottage cheese.

That stopped me snuffling to ask, "What do I put the cottage cheese on?"

"Don't put it on anything. Just eat it. Eat a bowl of it every day. Here, have an orange, too. But no cookies or candy, none of that sweet, starchy stuff. And no string beans. They're not good for you."

My eyes must have popped, but I guess I knew right that first day that you don't argue with Kate. I ate the cottage cheese—it doesn't really have any taste anyway—and I sure have always agreed with her about the string beans.

Off and on since then I've seen quite a lot of Kate. I'd pass her on the street, chirruping to some mangy old stray cat hiding under a car, and he'd always come out to be stroked. Sometimes there'd be a bunch of little kids dancing around jeering at her and calling her a witch. It made me feel real good and important to run them off.

Quite often I went with her to the A & P and helped her carry home the cat food and cottage cheese and fruit. She talks to herself all the time in the store, and if she thinks the peaches or melons don't look good that day, she shouts clear across the store to the manager. He comes across and picks her out an extra good one, just to keep the peace.

I introduced Kate to Mom, and they got along real well. Kate's leery of most people, afraid they'll make fun of her, I guess; my mom's not leery of people, but she's shy, and what with asthma and worrying about keeping me and Pop calmed down, she doesn't go out much or make dates with people. She and Kate would chat together in the stores or sitting on the stoop on a sunny day. Kate shook her head over Mom's asthma and said she'd get over it if she ate cottage cheese every day. Mom ate it for a while, but she put mayonnaise on it, which Kate says is just like poison.

The day of the fight with Pop about the Belafonte record it's cold and windy out and there are
no kids in sight. I slam my ball back and forth
against the wall where it says "No Ball Playing,"
just to limber up and let off a little spite, and then
I go over to see Kate.

Kate has a permanent cat named Susan and
however many kittens Susan happens to have just
had. It varies. Usually there are a few other tem-
porary stray kittens in the apartment, but I never
saw any father cat there before. Today Susan and
her kittens are under the stove, and Susan keeps
hissing at a big tiger-striped tomcat crouching
under the sofa. He turns his head away from her
and looks like he never intended to get mixed up
with family life. For a stray cat he's sleek and
healthy-looking. Every time he moves a whisker,
Susan hisses again, warningly. She believes in no
visiting rights for fathers.

Kate pours me some tea and asks what's doing.

"My pop is full of hot air, as usual," I say.

"Takes one to know one," Kate says, catching
me off base. I change the subject.

"How come the kittens' pop is around the house?
I never saw a full-grown tom here before."

"He saw me buying some cans of cat food, so he

followed me home. Susan isn't admitting she ever knew him or ever wants to. I'll give him another feed and send him on his way, I guess. He's a handsome young fellow." Kate strokes him between the ears, and he rotates his head. Susan hisses.

He starts to pull back farther under the sofa. Without stopping to think myself, or giving him time to, I pick him up. Susan arches up and spits. I can feel the muscles in his body tense up as he gets ready to spring out of my lap. Then he changes his mind and decides to take advantage of the lap. He narrows his eyes and gives Susan a bored look and turns his head to take me in. After he's sized me up, he pretends he only turned around to lick his back.

"Cat," I say to him, "how about coming home with me?"

"Hah!" Kate laughs. "Your pop will throw him out faster than you can say 'good old Jeff.' "

"Yeah-h?" I say it slowly and do some thinking. Taking Cat home had been just a passing thought, but right now I decide I'll really go to the mat with Pop about this. He can have his memories of good old Jeff and rabbit hunts, but I'm going to have me a tiger.

Aunt Kate gives me a can of cat food and a box of litter, so Cat can stay in my room, because I remember Mom probably gets asthma from animals, too. Cat and I go home.

Pop does a lot of shouting and sputtering when we get home, but I just put Cat down in my room, and I try not to argue with him, so I won't lose my temper. I promise I'll keep him in my room and sweep up the cat hairs so Mom won't have to.

As a final blast Pop says, "I suppose you'll get your exercise mouse hunting now. What are you going to name the noble animal?"

"Look, Pop," I explain, "I know he's a cat, he knows he's a cat, and his name is Cat. And even if you call him Admiral John Paul Jones, he won't come when you call, and he won't lick your hand, see?"

"He'd better not! And it's not my hand that's going to get licked around here in a minute," Pop snaps.

"All right, all right."

Actually, my pop sometimes jaws so long it'd be a relief if he did haul off and hit me, but he never does.

We call it a draw for that day, and I have Cat.

2
CAT AND THE UNDERWORLD

Cat makes himself at home in my room pretty easily. Mostly he likes to be up on top of something, so I put an old sweater on the bureau beside my bed, and he sleeps up there. When he wants me to wake up in the morning, he jumps and lands in the middle of my stomach. Believe me, cats don't always land lightly—only when they want to. Anything a cat does, he does only when he wants to. I like that.

When I'm combing my hair in the morning, sometimes he sits up there and looks down his nose at my reflection in the mirror. He appears to be taking inventory: "Hmm, buckteeth; sandy hair, smooth in front, cowlick in back; brown eyes, can't see in the dark worth a nickel; hickeys on the chin. Too bad."

I look back at him in the mirror and say, "O.K., black face, yellow eyes, and one white whisker. Where'd you get that one white whisker?"

He catches sight of himself in the mirror, and his tail twitches momentarily. He seems to know it's not really another cat, but his claws come out and he taps the mirror softly, just to make sure.

When I'm lying on the bed reading, sometimes he will curl up between my knees and the book. But after a few days I can see he's getting more and more restless. It gets so I can't listen to a record, for the noise of him scratching on the rug. I can't let him loose in the apartment, at least until we make sure Mom doesn't get asthma, so I figure I better reintroduce him to the great outdoors in the city. One nice Sunday morning in April we go down and sit on the stoop.

Cat sits down, very tall and neat and pear-shaped, and closes his eyes about halfway. He glances at the street like it isn't good enough for him. After a while, condescending, he eases down the steps and lies on a sunny, dusty spot in the middle of the sidewalk. People walking have to step around him, and he squints at them.

Then he gets up, quick, looks over his shoulder at nothing, and shoots down the stairs to the cellar. I take a look to see where he's going, and he is pacing slowly toward the backyard, head down, a tiger on the prowl. I figure I'll sit in the sun and finish my science-fiction magazine before I go after him.

When I do, he's not in sight, and the janitor tells me he jumped up on the wall and probably down into one of the other yards. I look around a while and call, but he's not in sight, and I go up to lunch. Along toward evening Cat scratches at the door and comes in, as if he'd done it all his life.

This gets to be a routine. Sometimes he doesn't even come home at night, and he's sitting on the doormat when I get the milk in the morning, looking offended.

"Is it my fault you stayed out all night?" I ask him.

He sticks his tail straight up and marches down the hall to the kitchen, where he waits for me to open the milk and dish out the cat food. Then he goes to bed.

One morning he's not there when I open the door, and he still hasn't showed up when I get back from school. I get worried and go down to talk to Butch.

"Wa-a-l," says Butch, "sometimes that cat sit and talk to me a little, but most times he go on over to Twenty-first Street, where he sit and talk to his lady friend. Turned cold last night, lot of buildings put on heat and closed up their basements. Maybe he got locked in somewheres."

"Which building's his friend live in?" I ask.

"Forty-six, the big one. His friend's a little black-and-white cat, sort of belongs to the night man over there. He feeds her."

I go around to Twenty-first Street and case Forty-six, which is a pretty fair-looking building with a striped awning and a doorman who saunters out front and looks around every few minutes.

While I'm watching, a grocery boy comes along pushing his cart and goes down some stairs into the basement with his carton of groceries. This gives me an idea. I'll give the boy time to get started up in the elevator, and then I'll go down in the basement and hunt for Cat. If someone comes along and gets sore, I can always play dumb.

I go down, and the coast is clear. The elevator's gone up, and I walk softly past and through a big room where the tenants leave their baby carriages and bicycles. After this the cellar stretches off into several corridors, lit by twenty-watt bulbs dangling from the ceiling. You can hardly see anything. The corridors go between wire storage cages, where the tenants keep stuff like trunks and old cribs and parakeet cages. They're all locked.

"Me-ow, meow, meow!" Unmistakably Cat, and angry.

The sound comes from the end of one corridor, and I fumble along, peering into each cage to try to see a tiger cat in a shadowy hole. Fortunately his eyes glow and he opens his mouth for another meow, and I see him locked inside one of the cages before I come to the end of the corridor. I don't know how he got in or how I'm going to get him out.

While I'm thinking, Cat's eyes flick away from me to the right, then back to me. Cat's not making any noise, and neither am I, but something is. It's just a tiny rustle, or a breath, but I have a creepy feeling someone is standing near us. Way down at the end of the cellar a shadow moves a

little, and I can see it has a white splotch—a
face. It's a man, and he comes toward me.

I don't know why any of the building men would
be way back there, but that's who I figure it is, so
I start explaining.

"I was just hunting for my cat . . . I mean, he's
got locked in one of these cages. I just want to get
him out."

The guy lets his breath out, slow, as if he's been
holding it quite a while. I realize he doesn't
belong in that cellar either, and he's been scared
of me.

He moves forward, saying "Sh-h-h" very quietly. He's taller than I am, and I can't see what he
really looks like, but I'm sure he's sort of a kid,
maybe eighteen or so.

He looks at the padlock on the cage and says,
"Huh, cheap!" He takes a paper clip out of his
pocket and opens it out, and I think maybe he has
a penknife, too, and next thing I know the padlock is open.

"Gee, how'd you do that?"

"Sh-h-h. A guy showed me how. You better get
your cat and scram."

Golly, I wonder, maybe the guy is a burglar, and
that gives me another creepy feeling. But would a

burglar be taking time out to get a kid's cat free?

"Well, thanks for the cat. See you around," I say.

"Sh-h-h. I don't live around here. Hurry up, before we both get caught."

Maybe he's a real burglar with a gun, even, I think, and by the time I dodge past the elevators and get out in the cold April wind, the sweat down my back is freezing. I give Cat a long lecture on staying out of basements. After all, I can't count on having a burglar handy to get him out every time.

Back home we put some nice jailhouse blues on the record player, and we both stretch out on the bed to think. The guy didn't really *look* like a burglar. And he didn't talk "dese and dose." Maybe real burglars don't all talk that way—only the ones on TV. Still, he sure picked that lock fast, and he was sure down in that cellar for some reason of his own.

Maybe I ought to let someone know. I figure I'll test Pop out, just casual like. "Some queer-looking types hanging around this neighborhood," I say at dinner. "I saw a tough-looking guy hanging around Number Forty-six this afternoon. Might have been a burglar, even."

I figure Pop'll at least ask me what he was

doing, and maybe I'll tell him the whole thing—
about Cat and the cage. But Pop says, "In case
you didn't know it, burglars do not all look like
Humphrey Bogart, and they don't wear signs."

"Thanks for the news," I say and go on eating
my dinner. Even if Pop does make me sore, I'm
not going to pass up steak and onions, which we
don't have very often.

However, the next day I'm walking along Twenty-
first Street and I see the super of Forty-six standing
by the back entrance, so I figure I'll try again. I say
to him, "Us kids were playing ball here yesterday,
and we saw a strange-looking guy sneak into your
cellar. It wasn't a delivery boy."

"Yeah? You sure it wasn't you or one of your
juvenile pals trying to swipe a bike? How come
you have to play ball right here?"

"I don't swipe bikes. I got one of my own. New.
A Raleigh. Better than any junk you got in there."

"What d'you know about what I got in there,
wise guy?"

"Aw, forget it." I realize he's just getting suspicious of me. That's what comes of trying to be a
big public-spirited citizen. I decide my burglar,
whoever he is, is a lot nicer than the super, and I
hope he got a fat haul.

Next day it looks like maybe he did just that. The local paper, *Town and Village,* has a headline: "Gramercy Park Cellar Robbed." I read down the article:

"The superintendent, Fred Snood, checked the cellar storage cages, after a passing youth hinted to him that there had been a robbery. He found one cage open and a suitcase missing. Police theorize that the youth may have been the burglar, or an accomplice with a guilty conscience or a grudge, and they are hunting him for questioning. Mr. Snood described him as about sixteen years of age, medium height, with a long 'ducktail' haircut, and wearing a heavy black sweater. They are also checking second-hand stores for the stolen suitcase."

The burglar stole a suitcase with valuable papers and some silver and jewelry in it. But the guy they were hunting for—I read the paragraph over and feel green. That's me. I get up and look in the mirror. In other circumstances I'd like being taken for sixteen instead of fourteen, which I am. I smooth my hair and squint at the back of it. The ducktail is fine.

Slowly I peel off my black sweater, which I wear practically all the time, and stuff it in my bottom drawer, under my bathing suit. But if I want to walk around the street without worrying about every cop, I'll have to do more than that. I put on a shirt and necktie and suit jacket and stick a cap on my head. I head uptown on the subway. At Sixty-eighth Street I get off and find a barbershop.

"Butch cut," I tell the guy.

"That's right. I'll trim you nice and neat. Get rid of all this stuff."

And while he chatters on like an idiot, I have to watch three months' work go snip, snip on the floor. Then I have to pay for it. At home I get the same routine. Pop looks at my Ivy League disguise and says, "Why, you may look positively human some day!"

Two days later I find out I could've kept my hair. *Town and Village* has a new story: "Nab Cellar Thief Returning Loot. 'Just A Bet,' He Says."

The story is pretty interesting. The guy I met in the cellar is named Tom Ransom, and he is nineteen and just sort of floating around in the city. He doesn't seem to have any family. The police kept a detective watching Number Forty-six, and pretty soon they see Tom walking along with the stolen suitcase. He drops it inside the delivery entrance and walks on, but the cop collars him. I suppose if it hadn't been for me shooting my big mouth off to the super, the police wouldn't have been watching the neighborhood. I feel sort of responsible.

The story in the paper goes on to say this guy was broke and hunting for a job, and some other guy dares him to snatch something out of a cellar and finally bets him ten dollars, so he does it. He gets out and finds the suitcase has a lot of stocks and legal papers and table silver in it, and he's scared stiff. So he figures to drop it back where it came from. The paper says he's held over to appear before some magistrate in Adolescent Court.

I wonder, would they send a guy to jail for that? Or if they turn him loose, what does he do? It must be lousy to be in this city without any family or friends.

At that point I get the idea I'll write him a letter. After all, Cat and I sort of got him into the soup. So I look up the name of the magistrate and spend about half an hour poring through the phone book, under "New York, City of," to get an address. I wonder whether to address him as "Tom" or "Mr. Ransom." Finally I write:

Dear Tom Ransom:

I am the kid you met in the cellar at Number Forty-six Gramercy, and I certainly thank you for unlocking that cage and getting my cat out. Cat is fine. I am sorry you got in trouble with the police. It sounds to me like you were only trying to return the stuff and do right. My father is a lawyer, if you would like one. I guess he's pretty good. Or if you would like to write me anyway, here is my address: 150 East 22 St. I read in the paper that your family don't live in New York, which is why I thought you might like someone to write to.

Yours sincerely,
Dave Mitchell

Now that I'm a free citizen again, I dig out my black sweater, look disgustedly at the butch haircut, and go out to mail my letter.

Later on I get into a stickball game again on Twenty-first Street. Cat comes along and sits up high on a stoop across the street, where he can watch the ball game and the tame dogs being led by on their leashes. That big brain, the super of Forty-six, is standing by the delivery entrance, looking sour as usual.

"Got any burglars in your basement these

days?" I yell to him while I'm jogging around the bases on a long hit.

He looks at me and my short haircut and scratches his own bald egg. "Where'd I see you?" he asks suspiciously.

"Oh—Cat and I, we get around," I say.

Nick and I have been friends pretty much since I can remember. Our mothers used to trade turns fetching us from kindergarten. Nick lives around the corner on Third Avenue, upstairs over the grocery store his old man runs. If anyone asked me *how come* we're friends, I couldn't exactly say. We're just together most of the time.

Neither of us is a real whiz at sports, but we used to roller-skate and play a little king and stickball and ride our bikes around exploring. One time when we were about ten, we rode way over to Twelfth Avenue at the Hudson River. where the *Queen Mary* docks. This is about the only time I remember my mom getting really angry. She said Pop ought to take my bike away from me, and he did, but only for about a week. Nick and I still ride bikes a lot. Otherwise we sit and do our homework or play chess and listen to records.

Another reason we're friends is because of this creepy little kid who lived down toward the corner, between me and Nick. He always tagged along, wanting to play with us, and of course in the end he always fouled up the game or fell down and started to cry. Then his big brother came rushing out, usually with another big guy along, and they figured they were entitled to beat us up for hurting little Joey.

After a while it looked to me as if Joey just worked as a lookout, and the minute me or Nick showed up on the block, one of the big guys came to run us off. They did little things like throwing sticks into our bike spokes and pretending it was just a joke. Nick and I used to plot all kinds of ways to get even with them, but in the end we mostly decided it was easier to walk around the block the long way to get to each other's houses.

I'm not much on fighting, and neither is Nick—
'specially not with guys bigger than us.

Summers, up in the country, the kids seem to be
all the time wrestling and punching, half for fun
and half not. If I walk past some strange kid my
age up there, he almost always tries to get me into
a fight. I don't get it. Maybe it's because sidewalks are uncomfortable for fighting, but we just
don't do much scrapping for fun. The only couple
of fights I ever had, I was real mad.

Come spring, Nick and I got restless hanging
around the street, with nothing to do but stickball
and baiting the super at Forty-six. It was so easy
to get him sore, it wasn't even fun. Cat stayed out
of that basement, but I wanted to get him really
out in the open, where he could chase squirrels or
something.

One day we rode our bikes up to Central Park.
I put Cat in a wicker hamper and tied it on the
back of my bike. He meowed a lot, and people on
the street would look at me and then do a double
take when they heard him.

We got up to Central Park and into a place they
call The Horseshoe, because the parking area is
that shape. I opened the lid a crack to look at Cat.
He hissed at me, the first time he ever did. I

looked around and thought, Gee, if I let him
loose, he could go anywhere, even over into the
woods, and I might never catch him. There were
a lot of hoody looking kids around, and I could
see if I ever left my bike a second to chase Cat,
they'd snatch the bike. So I didn't let Cat out, and
I wolfed my sandwich and we went home. Nick
was pretty disgusted.

Then we hit a hot Saturday, the first one in May,
and I got an idea. I find Nick and say, "Let's put
Cat and some sandwiches in the basket and hop
the subway out to Coney."

Nick says, "Why bring Cat? He wrecked the
last expedition."

"I like to take him places, and this won't be like
Central Park. No one's at Coney this time of year.
He can chase around on the beach and hunt sand
crabs."

"Why do I have to have a nut for a friend?" Nick
moans. "Well, anyway, I'm keeping my sandwich
in my pocket, not in any old cat basket."

"Who cares where you keep your crumby sandwich?"

So we went. Lots of people might think Coney
Island is ugly, with all the junky-looking booths
and billboards. But when you turn your back on

them and look out at the ocean, it's the same ocean as on a deserted beach. I kick off my shoes and stand with my feet in the ice water and the sun hot on my chest. Looking out at the horizon with its few ships and some sea gulls and planes overhead, I think: It's mine, all mine. I could go anywhere in the world, I could. Maybe I will.

Nick throws water down my neck. He only understands infinity on math papers. I let Cat out of the basket and strip off my splashed shirt and chase Nick along the edge of the water. No need to worry about Cat. He chases right along with us, and every time a wave catches his feet he hisses and hightails it up the beach. Then he rolls himself in the hot, dry sand and gets up and shakes. There are a few other groups of people dotted along the beach. A big mutt dog comes and sniffs Cat and gets a right and a left scratch to the nose. He yelps and runs for home. Cat discovers sand crabs. Nick and I roll around in the sand and wrestle, and after a while we get hungry, so we go back where we left the basket. Cat is content to let me carry him.

Three girls are having a picnic right near our basket. One yells to the others, "Hey, look! The guy went swimming with his cat!"

Cat jumps down, turns his back on them, and humps himself around on my sweater until he is settled for a nap. I turn my back on the girls, too, and look out at the ocean.

Still, it's not the same as it would have been a year ago. Then Nick and I would either have moved away from the girls or thrown sand at them.

We just sit and eat our sandwiches. Nick looks over at them pretty often and whispers to me how old do I think they are. I can't tell about girls. Some of the ones in our class at school look about twenty-five, but then you see mothers pushing baby carriages on the street who look about fifteen.

One of the girls catches Nick's eye and giggles. "Hi, there, whatcha watching?"

"I'm a bird watcher," says Nick. "Seen any birds?"

The girls drift over our way. The one that spoke first is a redhead. The one who seems to be the leader is a big blonde in a real short skirt and hair piled up high in a bird's nest. Maybe that's what started Nick bird-watching. The third girl is sort of quiet-looking, with brown hair, I guess.

"You want a couple of cupcakes? You can have

mine. I'm going on a diet," says the blonde.

"Thanks," says Nick. "I was thinking of going after some Cokes."

"Why waste time thinking? You might hurt your head," says the redhead.

The third girl bends down and strokes Cat between the ears very gently. She says, "What's his name?"

I explain to her about why Cat is Cat. She sits down and picks up a piece of seaweed to dangle over his nose. Cat makes a couple of sleepy swipes at it and then stretches luxuriously while she strokes him. The other kids get to talking, and we tell each other our names and where we go to school and all that stuff.

Then Nick gets back on the subject of going for Cokes. I don't really want to stay there alone with the girls, so I say I'll go. I tell Nick to watch Cat, and the girl who is petting him says, "Don't worry, I won't let him run away."

It's a good thing she's there, because by the time I get back with the Cokes, which no one offers to pay me back for, Nick and the other two girls are halfway down the beach. Mary—that's her name—says, "I never saw a cat at the beach before, but he seems to like it. Where'd you get him?"

"He's a stray. I got him from an old lady who's sort of a nut about cats. Come on, I'll see if I can get him to chase waves for you. He was doing it earlier."

We are running along in the waves when the other kids come back. The big blonde kicks up water at me and yells, "Race you!"

So I chase, and just as I'm going to catch up, she stops short so I crash into her and we both fall down. This seems to be what she had in mind, but I bet the other kids are watching and I feel silly. I roll away and get up and go back to Cat.

While we drink Cokes the blonde and the red-head say they want to go to the movies.

"What's on?" Nick asks.

"There's a Sinatra thing at the neighborhood," the blonde tells him, and he looks interested.

"I can't," I say. "I've got Cat. Besides, it's too late. Mom'd think I'd fallen into the subway."

"I told you that cat was a mistake," says Nick.

"Put him in the basket and call your mother and tell her your watch stopped," says the redhead. She comes over and trickles sand down my neck. "Come on, it'd be fun. We don't have to sit in the kids' section. We all look sixteen."

"Nah, I can't." I get up and shake the sand out.

Nick looks disgusted, but he doesn't want to stay alone. He says to the blonde, "Write me down your phone number, and we'll do it another day when this nut hasn't got his cat along."

She writes down the phone number, and the redhead pouts because I'm not asking for hers. The girls get ready to leave, and Mary pats Cat good-bye and waves to me. She says, "Bring him again. He's nice."

We get on the subway and Cat meows crossly at being shut in his basket. Nick pokes the basket with his toes.

"Shut up, nuisance," he says.

I actually get a letter back from Tom Ransom. It says: "Thanks for your letter. The Youth Board got me a room in the Y on Twenty-third Street. Maybe I'll come say Hello some day. They're going to help me get a job this summer, so I don't need a lawyer. Thanks anyway. Meow to Cat. Best, Tom."

I go over to Nick's house to show him the letter. I'd told him about Tom getting Cat out of the cellar and getting arrested, but Nick always acted like he didn't really believe it. So when he sees the letter, he has to admit Cat and I really got into something. Not everyone gets letters from guys who have been arrested.

One thing about Nick sort of gripes me. He has to think up all the plans. Anything I've done that he doesn't know about, he downgrades. Also, I always have to go to *his* house. He never comes to mine, except once in a coon's age when I have a new record I won't bring to his house because his machine stinks and he never buys a new needle.

It's not that I don't like his house. His mom is pretty nice, and boy, can she cook! Just an ordinary Saturday for lunch she makes pizza or real good spaghetti, and she has homemade cookies and nut cake sitting around after school. She also talks and waves her arms and shouts orders at us kids, but all good-natured-like, so we just kid her along and go on with what we're doing.

She's about the opposite of my mom. Pop does the shouting in our house, and except for the one hassle about bike-riding on Twelfth Avenue, Mom doesn't even tell me what to do much. She's quiet, and pretty often she doesn't feel good, so maybe I think more than most kids that I ought to do things her way without being told.

Also, my mom is always home and always ready to listen if you got something griping you, like when a teacher blames you for something you didn't do. Some kids I know, they have to phone a string of places to find their mother, and then she scolds them for interrupting her.

Mom likes to cook, and she gets up some good meals for holidays, but she doesn't go at it all the time, the way Nick's mother does. So maybe Nick doesn't come to my house because we haven't got all that good stuff sitting around. I don't think that's it, really, though. He just likes to be boss.

One day, a couple of weeks after we went to Coney, he does come along with me. We pick up a couple of Cokes and pears at his pop's store.

Cat is sitting on my front stoop, and he jumps down and rubs between my legs and goes up the stairs ahead of us.

"See? He knows when school gets out then it's time to eat. That's why I like to come home," I tell Nick.

We say "Hi" to Mom, and I get out the cat food while Nick opens his Coke. "You know those girls we ran into over on Coney Island?" he says.

"Yeah."

"Well, I got the blonde's phone number, so Sunday when I was hacking around with nothing to do, I called her up."

"Yeah? What for?"

"You stupid or something? To talk. So she
yacked away a good while, and finally I asked her
why didn't she come over next Saturday, we could
go to a movie or something."

"Yeah." I was working on my pear, a very juicy
one.

"That all you can say? So she says, well, she
might, if she can get her girl friend to come too,
but she doesn't want to come alone, and her
mother wouldn't let her anyway."

"Which one?"

"Which one what?"

"Which girl friend?"

"Oh. You remember, the other one we were kidding around with at the beach, the redhead. So I
said, O.K., I'd see if I could get you to come too.
I said I'd call her back."

"Hmp. I don't know."

"What d'you mean, you don't know?"

"How do I know if I like that girl? I hardly even
talked to her. Anyway, it sounds like a date. I
don't want a date. If they just happen to come
over, I guess it's all right."

"So shall I tell them it's O.K. for Saturday?"

"Hmm."

"It's nice you learned a new word."

"Do I have to pay for the girl at the movies?"

"Cheapskate. Maybe if you just stand around saying 'Hmm,' she'll buy her own. O.K.?"

"O.K. But this whole thing is your idea, and if it stinks it's going to be your fault."

"Boy, what an enthusiast! Come on, let's play a record and do the math."

Nick is better at math than I am, so I agree.

Saturday morning at ten o'clock Nick turns up at my house in a white shirt and slicked-down hair. Pop whistles. "On Saturday, yet! You got a girl or something?"

"Yessir!" says Nick, and he gives my T-shirt a dirty look. I go put a sweater over it and run a comb through my hair, but I'm hanged if I'll go out looking like this is a big deal.

"We're going to a movie down at the Academy," I tell my family.

"What's there?" Pop asks.

"A new horror show," says Nick. "And an old Disney."

"Is it really a new horror show?" I ask Nick, because I think I've seen every one that's been in town.

"Yup. Just opened. *The Gold Bug*. Some guy

wrote it—I mean in a book once—but it's supposed to be great. Make the girls squeal anyway. I love that."

"Hmm." I just like horror shows anyway, whether girls squeal or not.

"You'll be the life of the party with that 'Hmm' routine."

"It's *your* party." I shrug.

"Well, you could at least *try*."

We hang around the subway kiosk on Fourteenth Street, where Nick said he'd meet them. After half an hour they finally show up.

It's nice and sunny, and we see a crowd bunched up over in Union Square, so we wander over. A shaggy-haired, bearded character is making a speech all about "They," the bad guys. A lot of sleepy bums are sitting around letting the speech roll off their ears.

"What is he, a nut or something?" the blonde asks.

"A Commie, maybe," I say. "They're always giving speeches down here. Willie Sutton, the bank robber, used to sit down here and listen, too. That's where somebody put the finger on him."

The girls look at each other and laugh like crazy, as if I'd said something real funny. I catch

Nick's eye and glare. O.K., *I tried.* After this I'll stick to "Hmm."

A beard who is listening to the speech turns and glares at us and says, "Shush!"

"Aw, go shave yourself!" says Nick, and the girls go off in more hoots. Nick starts herding them toward Fourteenth Street, and I follow along.

At the Academy Nick goes up to the ticket window, and the girls immediately fade out to go read the posters and snicker together. I can see they're not figuring to pay for any tickets, so I cough up for two.

Nick and I try to saunter up to the balcony the way we always do, but the girls are giggling and dropping their popcorn, so the matron spots us and motions. "Down here!" She flashes her light in our eyes, and I feel like a convict while we get packed in with all the kids in the under-sixteen section.

Nick goes in first, then the blonde, then the red-head and me. The minute things start getting scary, she tries to grab me, but I stick my hands in my pockets and say, "Aw, it's just a picture." She looks disgusted.

The next scary bit, she tries to hang onto her

girl friend, but the blonde is already glued onto Nick. Redhead lets out a loud sigh, and I wish I hadn't ever got into this deal. I can't even enjoy the picture.

We suffer through the two pictures. The little kids make such a racket you can hardly hear, and the matron keeps shining the light in your eyes so you can't see. She shines it on the blonde, who is practically sitting in Nick's lap, and hisses at her to get back. I'm not going to do this again, ever.

We go out and Nick says, "Let's have a Coke." He's walking along with the blonde, and instead of walking beside me the redhead tries to catch hold of his other arm. This sort of burns me up. I mean, I don't really *like* her, but I paid for her and everything.

Nick shakes her off and calls over his shoulder to me, "Come on, chicken, pull your own weight!"

The girls laugh, on cue as usual, and I begin getting really sore. Nick got me into this. The least he can do is shut up.

We walk into a soda bar, and I slap down thirty cents and say, "Two Cokes, please."

"Hey, hey! The last of the big spenders!" says Nick. More laughter. I'd just as soon sock him right now, but I pick up my money and say, "O.K., wise guy, treat's on you." Nick shrugs and tosses down a buck as if he had hundreds of them.

The two girls drink their Cokes and talk across Nick. I finish mine in two or three gulps, and finally we can walk them to the subway. Nick is gabbing away about how he'll come out to Coney one weekend, and I'm standing there with my hands in my pockets.

"Goo'bye, Bashful!" coos the redhead to me, and the two of them disappear, cackling, down the steps. I start across Fourteenth Street as soon as the light changes, without bothering to look if Nick is coming. He can go rot.

Along Union Square he's beside me, acting as if everything is peachy fine dandy. "That was a great show. Pretty good fun, huh?"

I just keep walking.

"You sore or something?" he asks, as if he didn't know. I keep on walking.

"O.K., be sore!" he snaps. Then he breaks into a falsetto: "Goo'bye, Bashful!"

I let him have it before he's hardly got his mouth closed. He hits me back in the stomach and hooks one of his ankles around mine so we both fall down. It goes from bad to worse. He gets me by the hair and bangs my head on the sidewalk, so I twist and bite his hand. We're gouging and scratching and biting and kicking, because we're both so mad we can hardly see, and anyway no one ever taught us those Queensberry rules. There's no point in going into all the gory details. Finally two guys haul us apart. I have hold of Nick's shirt and it rips. Good. He's half crying, and he twists away from the guy that grabbed him and screams some things at me before darting across the avenue.

I'm standing panting and sobbing, and the guy holding me says, "You oughta be ashamed. Now go on home."

"Aw, you and your big mouth," I say, still mad enough to feel reckless. He throws a fake punch, but he's not really interested. He goes his way, and I go mine.

I must look pretty bad because a lot of people on the street shake their heads at me. I walk in the door at home, expecting the worst, but fortunately Mom is out. Pop just whistles through his teeth.

"That must have been quite a horror picture!" he says.

5

AROUND MANHATTAN

By the next weekend I no longer look like a fugitive from a riot. All week in school Nick and I get asked whether we got hit by a swinging door; then the fellows notice the two of us aren't speaking to each other, and they sort of sheer off the subject. Come Saturday, I sit on the stoop and wonder, what now? There are plenty of other kids in school I like, but they mostly live over in the project—Stuyvesant Town, that is. I've never bothered to hunt them up weekends because Nick's so much nearer.

Summer is coming on, though, and I've got to have someone to hang around with. This is the last Saturday before Memorial Day. Getting time for beaches and stuff. I suppose Nick and I might get together again, but not if he's going to be nuts about girls all the time.

A guy stops in front of the stoop, and Cat half opens his eyes in the sun and squints at him. The guy says, "You Dave Mitchell?"

"Huh? Yeah." I look up, surprised. I don't exactly recognize the guy, never having seen him in a clear light before. But from the voice I know it's Tom.

"Oh, hi!" I say. "Here's Cat. He's pretty handsome in daylight."

"Yeah, he looks all right, but what happened to you?"

"Me and a friend of mine got in a fight."

"With some other guys or what?"

"Nah. We had a fight with each other."

"Um, that's bad." Tom sits down and has sense enough to see there isn't anymore to say on that subject. "I start work Memorial Day, when the beaches open. Working in a filling station on the Belt Parkway in Brooklyn."

"Gee, that's a long way off. You going to live over there?"

"Yeah, they're going to get me a room in a Y in Brooklyn." Tom stretches restlessly and goes on: "I suppose you get sick of school and all, but it's rotten having nothing to do. I'd be ready to go nuts if I didn't get a job. I can't wait to start."

I think of asking him doesn't he have a home or something to go back to, but somehow I don't like to.

"Like today," Tom says. "I'd like to go somewhere. Do something. Got any ideas?"

"Um. I was sort of trying to think up something myself. Movies?"

Tom shakes himself. "No. I want to walk, or run, or throw something."

"There's a big park—sort of a woods—up near the Bronx. A kid told me about it. He said he found an Indian arrowhead there, but I bet he didn't. Inwood Park, it's called."

"How do you get there?"

"Subway, I guess."

"Let's go!" Tom stands up and wriggles his shoulders like he's Superman ready to take off.

"O.K. Wait a minute. I'll go tell Mom. Should I get some sandwiches?"

Tom looks surprised. "Sure, fine, if she doesn't mind."

I'm not worried about getting Mom to make sandwiches because she always likes to fix a little food for me. The thing is, ever since my fight with Nick, she's been clucking around me like the mother hen. Maybe she figures I got in some gang fight, so she keeps asking me where I'm going and who with. Also, I guess she noticed I don't go to Nick's after school anymore. I come right home. So she asks me do I feel all right. You can't win. Right now, I can see she's going to begin asking who is Tom and where did I meet him. It occurs to me there's an easy way to take care of this.

I turn around to Tom again. "Say, how about you come up and I'll introduce you to Mom? Then she won't start asking me a lot of questions."

"You mean I *look* respectable, at least?"

"Sure."

We go up to the apartment, and Mom asks if we'd like some cold drinks or something. I tell her I ran into Tom when he helped me hunt for Cat around Gramercy Park, which is almost true, and that he sometimes plays stickball with us, which isn't really true but it could be. Mom gets us some orangeade. She usually keeps something like that in the icebox in summer, because she thinks Cokes are bad for you.

"Do you live around here?" she asks Tom.

"No, ma'am," says Tom firmly. "I live at the Y. I've got a summer job in a filling station over in Brooklyn, starting right after Memorial Day."

"That's fine," Mom says. "I wish Davey could get a job. He gets so restless with nothing to do in the summer."

"Aw, Mom, forget it! You got to fill in about six-hundred working papers if you're under sixteen.

"Listen, Mom, what I came up for—we thought we'd make some sandwiches and go up to Inwood Park."

"Inwood? Where's that?" So I explain to her about the Indian arrowheads, and we get out the classified phone book and look at the subway map, which shows there's an IND train that goes right to it.

"I get sort of restless myself, with nothing to do," says Tom. "We just figured we'd do a little exploring around in the woods and get some exercise."

"Why, yes, that seems like a good idea." Mom looks at him and nods. She seems to have decided he's reliable, as well as respectable.

I see there's some leftover cold spaghetti in the icebox, and I ask Mom to put it in sandwiches.

She thinks I'm cracked, but I did this once before, and it's good, 'specially if there's plenty of meat and sauce on the spaghetti. We take along a bag of cherries, too.

"Thanks, Mom. Bye. I'll be back before supper."

"Take care," she says. "No fights."

"Don't worry. We'll stay out of fights," says Tom quite seriously.

We go down the stairs, and Tom says, "Your mother is really nice."

I'm sort of surprised—kids don't usually say much about each other's parents. "Yeah, Mom's O.K. I guess she worries about me and Pop a lot."

"It must be pretty nice to have your mother at home," he says.

That kind of jolts me, too. I wonder where his mother and father are, whether they're dead or something; but again, I don't quite want to ask. Tom isn't an easy guy to ask questions. He's sort of like an island, by himself in the ocean.

We walk down to Fourteenth Street and over to Eighth Avenue, about twelve blocks; after all, exercise is what we want. The IND trains are fast, and it only takes about half an hour to get up to Inwood, at 206th Street. The park is right close, and it is real woods, although there are paved walks around through it. We push uphill and get in a grassy meadow, where you can see out over the Hudson River to the Palisades in Jersey. It's good and hot, and we flop in the sun. There aren't many other people around, which is rare in New York.

"Let's eat lunch," says Tom. "Then we can go hunting arrowheads and not have to carry it."

He agrees the spaghetti sandwich is a great invention.

I wish the weather would stay like this more of the year—good and sweaty hot in the middle of the day, so you feel like going swimming, but cool enough to sleep at night. We lie in the sun awhile after lunch and agree that it's too bad there isn't an ocean within jumping-in distance. But there isn't, and flies are biting the backs of our necks, so we get up and start exploring.

We find a few places that you might conceivably call caves, but they've been well picked over for arrowheads, if there ever were any. That's the trouble in the city: anytime you have an idea, you find out a million other people had the same idea first. Along in mid-afternoon, we drift down toward the subway and get Cokes and ice cream before we start back.

I don't really feel like going home yet, so I think a minute and study the subway map inside the car. "Hey, as long as we're on the subway anyway, we could go on down to Cortlandt Street to the Army-Navy surplus store. I got to get a knapsack before summer."

"O.K." Tom shrugs. He's staring out the window and doesn't seem to care where he goes.

"I got a great first-aid survival kit there. Disinfectant and burn ointment and bug dope and bandages, in a khaki metal box that's waterproof, and it was only sixty-five cents."

"Hmm. Just what I need for survival on the sidewalks of New York," says Tom. I guess he's kidding, in a sour sort of way. If you haven't got a family around, though, survival must take more than a sixty-five-cent kit.

The store is a little way from the nearest subway stop, and we walk along not saying much. Tom looks alive when he gets into the store, though, because it really is a great place. They've got arctic explorers' suits and old hand grenades and shells and all kinds of rifles, as well as some really cheap, useful clothing. They don't mind how long you mosey around. In the end I buy a belt pack and canteen, and Tom picks up some skivvy shirts and socks that are only ten cents each. They're secondhand, I guess, but they look all right.

We walk over to the East Side subway, which is only a few blocks away down here because the island gets so narrow. Tom says he's never seen Wall Street, where all the tycoons grind their money machines. The place is practically deserted now, being late Saturday afternoon, and it's like walking through an empty cathedral. You can make echoes.

We take the subway, and Tom walks along home with me. It seems too bad the day's over. It was a pretty good day, after all.

"So long, kid," Tom says. "I'll send you a card from Beautiful Brooklyn!"

"So long." I wave, and he starts off. I wish he didn't have to go live in Brooklyn.

6

AND BROOKLYN

You can't really stay sore at a guy you've known all your life, especially if he lives right around the corner and goes to the same school. Anyhow, one hot Saturday morning Nick turns up at my house as if nothing had ever happened and says do I want to go swimming, because the Twenty-third Street pool's open weekends now.

After that we go back to playing ball on the street in the evenings and swimming sometimes on weekends. One Saturday his mother tells me he went to Coney Island. He didn't ask me to go

along, which is just as well, because I wouldn't
have. I don't hang around his house after school
much anymore, either. School lets out, and there's
the Fourth of July weekend, when we go up to
Connecticut, and pretty soon after that Nick goes
off to a camp his church runs. Pop asks me if I
want to go to a camp a few weeks, but I don't. Life
is pretty slow at home, but I don't feel like all that
organization.

I think Tom must have forgotten about me and
found a gang his own age when I get a postcard
from him: "Dear Dave, The guy I work for is a
creep, and all the guys who buy gas from him are
creeps, so it's great to be alive in Beautiful
Brooklyn! Wish you were here, but you're lucky
you're not. Best, Tom."

It's hard to figure what he means when he says
a thing. However, I got nothing to do, so I might
as well go see. He said he was going to work in a
filling station on the Belt Parkway, and there
can't be a million of them.

I don't say anything too exact to Mom about
where I'm going, because she gets worried about
me going too far, and besides I don't really know
where I'm going.

Brooklyn, what a layout. It's not like Manhattan,

which runs pretty regularly north and south, with decent square blocks. You could lose a million friends in Brooklyn, with the streets all running in circles and angles, and the people all giving you cockeyed directions. What with no bikes allowed on parkways, and skirting around crumby looking neighborhoods, it takes me at least a week of expeditions to find the right part of the Belt Parkway to start checking the filling stations.

I wheel my bike across the parkway, but even so some cop yells at me. You'd think a cop could find a crime to get busy with.

On a real sticky day in July I wheel across to a station at Thirty-fourth Street, and nobody yells at me, and I go over to the air pump and fiddle with my tires. A car pulls out after it gets gas, and there's Tom.

"Hi!" I say.

Tom half frowns and quick looks over his shoulder to see if his boss is around, I guess, and then comes over to the air pump.

"How'd you get way out here?" he says.

"On the bike. I got your postcard, and I figured I could find the filling station."

He relaxes and grins. I feel better. He says, "You're a crazy kid. How's Cat?"

But just then the boss has to come steaming up. "What d'ya want, kid? No bikes allowed on the parkway."

I start to say I'm just getting air, but Tom speaks up. "It's all right. I know him."

"Yeah? I told you, keep kids out of here!" The guy manages to suggest that kids Tom knows are probably worse than any other kind. He motions me off like a stray dog. I don't want to get Tom in any trouble, so I get going. At the edge of the parkway I wave. "So long. Write me another post-card."

Tom raises a hand briefly, but his face looks closed, like nothing was going to get in or out.

I pedal slowly and hotly back through the tangle of Brooklyn and figure, well, that's a week's research wasted. I still don't know where Tom lives, so I don't know how I can get a hold of him again. Anyway, how do I know he wants to be bothered with me? He looked pretty fed up with everything.

So long as I got nothing else to do, the next week I figure I'll get public-spirited at home. I paint the kitchen for Mom, which isn't so bad, but moving all those silly dishes and pots and scrumy little spice cans can drive you wild. I only break one good vase and a bottle of salad oil. Salad oil and broken glass are great. In the afternoons I go to the swimming pool and learn to do a jackknife and a backflip, so Pop will think I am growing up to be a Real American Boy. Also, you practically have to learn to dive so you can use the diving pool, because the swimming pool is so jam-packed with screaming sardines you can't move in it.

Evenings Cat and I play records, or we go to see Aunt Kate and drink iced tea. One weekend my real aunt comes to visit and sleeps in my room, so I go to stay with Aunt Kate, and I pretty near turn into cottage cheese.

I've about settled into this dull routine when Mom surprises me by handing me a postcard one morning. It's from Tom: "Day off next Tuesday. If you feel like it, meet me near the aquarium at Coney Island about nine in the morning, before it's crowded."

So that week drags by till Tuesday, and there I am at Coney Island bright and early. Tom is easy enough to find, pacing up and down the boardwalk like a tiger. We say "Hi" and so forth, and I'm all ready to take a run for the water, but he keeps snapping his fingers and looking up and down the boardwalk.

Finally he says, "There's a girl I used to know pretty well. I didn't see her for a while till last week, and we got in an argument, and I guess she's mad. I wrote and asked her to come swimming today, but maybe she's not coming."

I figure it out that I'm there as insurance against the girl not showing up, but I don't mind. Anyhow, she does show up. It can't have been too much of an argument they had, because she acts pretty friendly.

Tom introduces us. Her name is Hilda and a last name that'd be hard to spell—Swedish maybe—and she's got a wide, laughing kind of mouth and a big coil of yellow hair in a bun on top of her head, and a mighty good figure. She asks me where I ran into Tom, and we tell her all about Cat and the cellar at Number Forty-six, and I tell them both about my Ivy-League haircut, which I had never explained to anyone before. They get a laugh out of that, and then she asks him about the filling-station job, and he says it stinks.

I figure they could get along without me for a while, so I go for a swim and wander down the beach a ways and eat a hot dog and swim some more. When I come back, I see Tom and Hilda just coming out of the water, so I join them. Hilda says, "Come have a Coke. Tom says he's got to try swimming to France just once more."

I don't know just what she means, but we go get Cokes and come back and stretch out in the sun. She asks me do I want a smoke, and I say No. It's nice to be asked, though. We watch Tom, who is swimming out past all the other people. I wish I'd gone with him. I say, "Lifeguard's going to whistle him in pretty soon. He's out past all the others."

Hilda lets out a breath and snorts, "He'll always go till they blow the whistle. Always got to go farther than anyone else."

I don't know what to say to that, so I don't say anything.

Hilda goes on: "I used to wait tables in a restaurant down near Washington Square. Tom and a lot of the boys from NYU came in there. Sometimes the day before an exam he'd be sitting around for hours, buying people Cokes and acting as if he hadn't a care in the world. Some other times, for no reason anyone could tell, he'd sit in a corner and stir his coffee like he was going to make a hole in the cup."

"Tom was at NYU?" I ask. I don't know where I thought he'd been before he turned up in the cellar. I guess I never thought.

"Sure," Hilda says. "He was in the Washington Square College for about a year and a half. He lived in a dormitory uptown, but I used to see him in the restaurant, and then fairly often we had dates after I got off work. He has people out in the Midwest somewhere—a father and a stepmother. He was always sour and close-mouthed about them, even before he got thrown out of NYU. Now he won't even write them."

This is a lot of information to take in all at once and leaves a lot of questions unanswered. The first one that comes into my head is this: "How come he got thrown out of NYU?"

"Well, it makes Tom so sore, he's never really told me a plain, straight story. It's all mixed up with his father. I think his father wrote him not to come home at Christmas vacation, for some reason. Tom and a couple of other boys who were left in the dormitory over the holidays got horsing around and had a water fight. The college got huffy and wrote the parents, telling them to pay up for damages. The other parents were pretty angry, but they stuck behind their kids and paid up. Tom just never heard from his father. Not a line.

"That was when Tom began coming into the restaurant looking like thunder. The college began needling him for the water-fight damages, as well as second-semester tuition. He took his first exam, physics, and got an A on it. He's pretty smart.

"He still didn't hear anything from home. He took the second exam, French, and thought he flunked it. That same afternoon he went into the office and told the dean he was quitting, and he packed his stuff and left. I didn't see him again till a week ago. I didn't know if he'd got sick of me, or left town, or what.

"He says he wrote his father that he had a good job, and they could forget about him. Then he broke into that cellar on a dare or for kicks.

"So here we are. What do we do next?"

Hilda looks at me—me, age fourteen—as if I might actually know, and it's kind of unnerving. Everyone I know, their life goes along in set periods: grade school, junior high, high school, college, and maybe getting married. They don't really have to think what comes next.

I say cautiously, "My pop says a kid's got to go to college now to get anywhere. Maybe he ought to go back to school."

"You're so right, Grandpa," she says, and I would have felt silly, but she has a nice friendly laugh. "I wish I could persuade him to go back.

But it's not so easy. I guess he's got to get a job and go to night school, if they'll accept him. He won't ask his father for money."

"You two got my life figured out?" Tom has come up behind us while we were lying in the sand on our stomachs. "I just hope that sour grape at the filling station gives me a good recommendation so I can get another job. The way he watches his cash register, you'd think I was Al Capone."

We talk a bit, and then Hilda gets up and says she's going to the ladies' room. She doesn't act coy about it, the way most girls do when they're sitting with guys. She just leaves.

"How do you like Hilda?" Tom asks, and again I'm sort of surprised, because he acts like he really wants my opinion. "She's nice," I say.

"Yeah." Tom suddenly glowers, as if I'd said I *didn't* like her. "I don't know why she wastes her time on me. I'll never be any use to her. When her family hears about me, I'll get the boot."

"I could ask my pop. You know, I told you he's a lawyer. Maybe he'd know how you go about getting back into college or getting a job or something."

Tom laughs, an unamused bark. "Maybe he'll tell you to quit hanging around with jerks that get in trouble with the cops."

This is a point, all right. Come to think, I don't know why I said I'd ask Pop anyway. I usually make a point of not letting his nose into my personal affairs, because I figure he'll just start bossing me around. However, I certainly can't do anything for Tom on my own.

I say, "I'll chance it. The worst he ever does is talk. One time he made a federal case out of me buying a Belafonte record he didn't like. Another time playing ball I cracked a window in a guy's Cadillac, and Pop acted like he was going to sue the guy for owning a Cadillac. You just never know."

Tom says, "With my dad, you *know*: I'm wrong."

Hilda comes back just then. She snaps, "If he's such a drug on the market, why don't you shut up and forget about him?"

"O.K., O.K.," says Tom.

The beach is getting filled up by now, so we pull on our clothes and head for the subway. Tom and Hilda get off in Brooklyn, and I go on to Union Square.

After dinner that night Mom is washing the dishes and Pop is reading the paper, and I figure I might as well dive in.

"Pop," I say, "there's this guy I met at the beach.

Well, really I mean I met him this spring when I was hunting for Cat, and this guy was in the cellar at Forty-six Gramercy, and he got caught and . . ."

"Wha-a-a-t?" Pop puts down his paper and takes off his glasses. "Begin again."

So I give it to him again, slow, and with explanations. I go through the whole business about the filling station and Hilda and NYU, and I'll say one thing for Pop, when he finally settles down to listen, he listens. I get through, and he puts on his reading glasses and goes to look out the window.

"Do you have this young man's name and address, or is he just Tom from The Cellar?"

I'd just got it from Tom when we were at the beach. He's at a Y in Brooklyn, so I tell Pop this.

Pop says, "Tell him to call my office and come in to see me on his next day off. Meanwhile, I'll bone up on City educational policies in regard to juvenile delinquents."

He says this perfectly straight, as if there'd be a book on the subject. Then he goes back to his newspaper, so I guess that closes the subject for now.

"Thanks, Pop," I say and start to go out.

"Entirely welcome," says Pop. As I get to the door, he adds, "If that cat of yours makes a practice of introducing you to the underworld in other people's cellars, we can do without him. We probably can anyway."

7

SURVIVAL

Cat hadn't got me into any more cellars, but I can't honestly say he'd been sitting home tending his knitting—not him.

One hot morning I went to pick up the milk outside our door, and Cat was sleeping there on the mat. He didn't even look up at me. After I scratched his ears and talked to him some, he got up and hobbled into the house.

I put him up on my bed, under the light, for inspection. One front claw was torn off, which is why he was limping, his left ear was ripped, and there was quite a bit of fur missing here and there. He curled up on my bed and didn't move all day.

I came and looked at him every few hours and wondered if I ought to take him to a vet. But he seemed to be breathing all right, so I went away and thought about it some more. Come night, I pushed him gently to one side, wondering what I better do in the morning.

Well, in the morning Cat wakes up, stretches, yawns, and drops easily down off the bed and walks away. He still limps a little, but otherwise he acts like nothing had happened. He just wants to know what's for breakfast.

"You better watch out. One day you'll run into a cat that's bigger and meaner than you," I tell him.

Cat continues to wait for breakfast. He is not impressed.

But I'm worried. Suppose some big old cat chews him up and he's hurt too bad to get home? After breakfast I take him out in the backyard for a bit, and then I shut him in my room and go over to consult Aunt Kate.

She sets me up with the usual iced tea and dish of cottage cheese.

"I had breakfast already. What do I need with cottage cheese?"

"Eat it. It's good for you."

So I eat it, and then I start telling her about Cat. "He came home all chewed up night before last. I'm afraid some night he's not going to make it."

"Right," says Kate. She's not very talky, but I'm sort of surprised. I expected she'd tell me to quit worrying, Cat can take care of himself. She starts pulling Susan's latest kittens out from under the sofa and sorting them out as if they were ribbons: one gray, two tiger, one yellow, one calico.

"So what you going to do?" she shoots at me, shoveling the kittens back to Susan.

"I—uh—I dunno. I thought maybe I ought to try to keep him in nights."

"Huh. Don't know much, do you?" she says. "Well, so I'll tell you. Your Cat has probably fathered a few dozen kittens by now, and once a cat's been out and mated, you can't keep him in. You got to get him altered. Then he won't want to go out so much."

"Altered?"

"Fixed. Castrated is the technical word. It's a two-minute operation. Cost you three dollars. Take him to Speyer Hospital—big new building up on First Avenue."

"You mean get him fixed so he's not a real

tomcat anymore? The heck with that! I don't want him turned into a fat old cushion cat!"

"He won't be," she says. "But if it makes you happier, let him get killed in a cat fight. He's tough. He'll last a year or two. Suit yourself."

"Ah, you're screwy! You and your cottage cheese!" Even as I say it I feel a little guilty. But I feel mad and mixed up, and I fling out the door. It's the first time I ever left Kate's mad. Usually I leave *our* house mad and go to Kate.

Now I got nowhere to go. I walk along, cussing and fuming and kicking pebbles. I come to an air-conditioned movie and go up to the window.

The phony blonde in the booth looks at me and sneers, "You're not sixteen. We don't have a children's section in this theater." She doesn't even ask. She just says it. It's a great world. I go home. There's no one there but Cat, so I turn the record player up full blast.

Pop comes home in one of his unexpected fits of generosity that night and takes us to the movies. Cat behaves himself and stays around home and our cellar for a while, so I stop worrying. But it doesn't last long.

As soon as his claw heals, he starts sashaying off again. One night I hear cats yowling out back and I go out with a bucket of water and douse them and bring Cat in. There's a pretty little tiger cat, hardly more than a kitten, sitting on the fence licking herself, dry and unconcerned. Cat doesn't speak to me for a couple of days.

One morning Butch, the janitor, comes up and knocks on our door. "You better come down and look at your cat. He got himself mighty chewed up. Most near dead."

I hurry down, and there is Cat sprawled in a corner on the cool cement floor. His mouth is half open, and his breath comes in wheezes, like he has asthma. I don't know whether to pick him up or not.

Butch says, "Best let him lie."

I sit down beside him. After a bit his breath comes easier and he puts his head down. Then I see he's got a long, deep claw gouge going from his shoulder down one leg. It's half an inch open, and anyone can see it won't heal by itself.

Butch shakes his head. "You gotta take him to the veteran, sure. That's the cat doctor."

"Yeah," I say, not correcting him. It's not just the gash that's worrying me. I remember what Aunt Kate said, and it gives me a cold feeling in the stomach: In the back-alley jungle he'd last a year, maybe two.

Looking at Cat, right now, I know she's right. But Cat's such a—well, such a *cat*. How can I take him to be whittled down?

I tell Butch I'll be back down in a few minutes, and I go upstairs. Mom's humming and cleaning in the kitchen. I wander around and stare out the window awhile. Finally I go in the kitchen and stare into the icebox, and then I tell Mom about the gash in Cat's leg.

She asks if I know a vet to take him to.

"Yeah, there's Speyer. It's a big, new hospital—good enough for people, even—with a view of the East River. The thing is, Mom, Cat keeps going off and fighting and getting hurt, and people tell me I ought to get him altered."

Mom wets the sponge and squeezes it out and polishes at the sink, and I wonder if she knows what I'm talking about because I don't really know how to explain it any better.

She wrings the sponge out, finally, and sits down at the kitchen table.

She says, "Cat's not a free wild animal now, and he wouldn't be even if you turned him loose. He belongs to *you*, so you have to do whatever is best for *him*, whether it's what you'd like or not. Ask the doctor and do what he says."

Mom puts it on the line, all right. It doesn't make me feel any better about Cat. She takes five dollars out of her pocketbook and gives it to me.

I get out the wicker hamper and go down to the cellar and load Cat in. He meows, a low resentful rumble, but he doesn't try to get away.

Cat in the hamper is no powder puff, and I get pretty hot walking to the bus, and then from the bus stop to the animal hospital. I get there and wait, and dogs sniff at me, and I fill in forms. The lady asks me if I can afford to pay, and with Mom's five bucks and four of my own, I say Yes.

The doctor is a youngish guy, but bald, in a white shirt like a dentist's. I put Cat on the table in front of him. He says, "So why don't you stay out of fights, like your mommy told you?"

I relax a bit and smile, and he says, "That's better. Don't worry. We'll take care of tomcat. I suppose he got this gash in a fight?"

"Yeah."

"He been altered?"

"No."

"How old is he?"

"I don't know. He was a stray. I've had him almost a year."

All the time he's talking, the doctor is soothing

Cat and looking him over. He goes on stroking him and looks up at me. "Well, son, one of these days he's going to get in one fight too many. Shall we alter him the same time we sew up his leg?"

So there it is. I can't seem to answer right away. If the doctor had argued with me, I might have said No. But he just goes on humming and stroking. Finally he says, "It's tough, I know. Maybe he's got a right to be a tiger. But you can't keep a tiger for a pet."

I say, "O.K."

An attendant takes Cat away, and I go sit in the waiting room, feeling sweaty and cold all over. They tell me it'll be a couple of hours, so I go out and wander around a lot of blocks I never saw before and drink some Cokes and sit and look up at the Fifty-ninth Street Bridge to Queens.

When I go back for him, Cat looks the same as ever, except for a bandage all up his right front leg. The doctor tells me to come back Friday and he'll take out the stitches.

Mom sees me come in the door, and I guess I look pretty grim, because she says, "Cat will be all right, won't he, dear?"

"Yes." I go past her and down into my room and let Cat out of the basket and then bury my head under the pillow. I'm not exactly ashamed of crying, but I don't want Mom to hear.

After a while I pull my head out. Cat is lying there beside me, his eyes half open, the tip end of his tail twitching very slowly. I rub my eyes on the back of his neck and whisper to him, "I'm sorry. Be tough, Cat, anyway, will you?"

Cat stretches and hops off the bed on his three good legs.

8

WEST SIDE STORY

The regular park man got sunstroke or something, so I earned fourteen dollars raking and mowing in Gramercy Park in the middle of August. Gramercy Park is a private park. You have to own a key to get in, so the city doesn't take care of it.

Real paper money, at this time of year especially, is very cheering. I head up to Sam Goody's to see what records he's got on sale and what characters are buying them. Maybe I'll buy something, maybe not, but as long as I've got money in my pocket, I don't feel like the guy is glaring at me for taking up floor space.

Along the way I walk through the library, the big one at Forty-second Street. You go in by the lions on Fifth Avenue, and there's all kinds of pictures and books on exhibit in the halls, and you walk through to the back, where you can take out books. It's nice and cool, and nobody glares at you unless you either make a lot of noise or go to sleep. I can take books out of here and return them at the Twenty-third Street branch, which is handy.

Sam Goody's is air-conditioned, so it's cool too. There are always several things playing on different machines you can listen to. Almost the most fun is watching the people: little, fat, bald guys buying long-haired classical music, and thin, shaggy beatniks listening to the jazz.

I go to check if there are any bargains in the Kingston or Belafonte division. There's a girl standing there reading the backs of records, but I don't really catch a look at more than her shoes— little red flats they are. After a bit she reaches for a record over my head and says, "Excuse me."

"Sure." Then we catch each other's eye and both say, "Oh. Gee, hello."

Well, we're both pretty surprised, because this is the girl I met out at Coney Island that day with Nick when I had Cat with me, and now we're both a long way from Coney Island. This girl isn't one of the two giggly ones. It's the third, the one that liked Cat.

We've both forgotten each other's names, so we begin over with that. I ask her what she's been doing, and she's been at Girl Scout camp a few weeks, and then she earned some money baby-sitting. So she came to think about records, like me. I tell her I've been at Coney once this summer, and I looked around for her, which is true, because I did.

"It's a big place," she says, smiling.

"Say, you live out there, don't you? How come you get all the way in here by yourself? Doesn't your mom get in a flap? Mine would, if she knew I was going to Coney alone."

Mary says, "I came in with Mom. Some friend of hers has a small art exhibition opening. She said I could go home alone. After all, she knows I'm not going to get lost."

I say, "Gee, it'd be great to have a mother that didn't worry about you all the time."

"Oh, Mom worries." Mary giggles. "You should

have heard her when I said I liked *Gone With the Wind* and I didn't like *Anna Karenina*. I pretty nearly got disowned."

"What does she think about science fiction?" I ask, and Mary makes a face, and we both laugh.

I go on. "Well, my mom doesn't care what I read. She worries about what I eat and whether my feet are wet, and she always seems to think I'm about to kill myself. It's a nuisance, really."

Mary looks solemn all of a sudden. She says slowly, "I think maybe it'd be nice. I mean to have someone worrying about whether you're comfortable and all. Instead of just picking your brains all the time."

This seems to exhaust the subject of our respective mothers, and Mary picks up the record of *West Side Story* and says, "Gee, I'd like to see that. Did you?"

I say No, and to tell the truth I hadn't hardly heard of it.

"I read a book about him. It was wonderful," she says.

"Who?"

"Bernstein. The man who wrote it."

"What's *West Side Story* about, him?" I ask cautiously.

"No, no—he wrote the music. It's about some kids in two gangs, and there's a lot of dancing, and then there's a fight and this kid gets—well, it isn't a thing you can tell the story of very well. You have to see it."

This gives me a very simple idea.

"Why don't we?" I say.

"Huh?"

"Go see it. Why not? We got money."

"So we do," she says slowly. "You think they'll let us in, I mean being under sixteen?"

You know, this is the first girl I really ever talked to that talks like a person, not trying to be cute or something.

We walk around to the theater, and being it's Wednesday, there's a matinee about to start. The man doesn't seem to be one bit worried about taking our money. No wonder. It's two dollars and ninety cents each. So we're inside with our tickets before we've hardly stopped to think.

Suddenly Mary says, "Oops! I better call Mom! Let's find out what time the show is over."

We do, and Mary phones. She says to me, "I just told her I was walking past *West Side Story* and found I could get a ticket. I didn't say anything about you."

"Why, would she mind?"

Mary squints and looks puzzled. "I don't know. I just really don't know. It never happened before."

We go in to the show, and she is right, it's terrific. I hardly ever went to a live show before, except a couple of children's things and something by Shakespeare Pop took me to that was very confusing. But this *West Side Story* is clear as a bell.

We have an orangeade during intermission, and I make the big gesture and pay for both of them. Mary says, "Isn't it wonderful! I just happened to meet you at the beach, and then I meet you at Goody's, and we get to see this show that I've wanted to go to for ages. None of my friends at school want to spend this much money on a show."

"It's wonderful," I say. "After it's over, I'm going back to buy the record."

So after the show we buy it, and then we walk along together to the subway. I'll have to get off at the first stop, Fourteenth Street, and she'll go on to Coney, the end of the line.

It's hard to talk on the subway. There's so much noise you have to shout, which is hard if you don't know what to say. Anyway, you can't ask a girl for her phone number shouting on the subway. At least I can't.

I'm not so sure about the phone-number business either. I sort of can't imagine calling up and saying, "Oh, uh, Mary, this is Dave. You want to go to a movie or something, huh?" It sounds stupid, and I'd be embarrassed. What she said, it's true—it's sort of wonderful the way we just ran into each other twice and had so much fun.

So I'm wondering how I can happen to run into her again. Maybe the beach, in the fall. Let's see, a school holiday—Columbus Day.

The train is pulling into Fourteenth Street. I shout, "Hey, how about we go to the beach again this fall? Maybe Columbus Day?"

"O.K.!" she shouts. "Columbus Day in the morning."

"Columbus Day in the morning" sounds loud and clear because by then the subway has stopped. People snicker, and Mary blushes.

"So long," I say, and we both wave, and the train goes.

9
FATHERS

That operation didn't make as much difference to Cat as you might think. I took him back to the clinic to get the stitches out of his leg and the bandages off. A few nights later I heard yowls coming up from the backyard. I went down and pulled him out of a fight. He wasn't hurt yet, but he sure was right back in there pitching. He seems to have a standing feud with the cat next door.

However, he's been coming home nights regularly, and sometimes in the cool part of the morning he'll sit out on the front stoop with me. He sits on a pillar about six feet above the sidewalk, and I sit on the steps and play my transistor and read.

Every time a dog gets walked down the street under Cat's perch, he gathers himself up in a ball, as if he were going to spring. Of course, the poor dog never knows it was about to be pounced on and wags on down the street. Cat lets his tail go to sleep then and sneers.

Between weathercasts I hear him purring, loud rumbly purrs, and I look up and see Tom there, stroking Cat's fur up backward toward his ears. Tom is looking out into the street and sort of whistling without making any sound.

"Gee, hi!" I say.

"Hi, too," he says. He strokes Cat back down the right way, gives him a pat, and sits down. "I just been down to see your dad. He's quite a guy."

"Huh-h-h? You got sunstroke or something? Didn't he read you about ten lectures on Healthy Living, Honest Effort, Baseball, and Long Walks with a Dog?"

"No-o-o." Tom grins, but then he sits and stares out at the street again, so I wait.

"You know," he says, "you give me an idea. *You* talk like *your* dad is a real pain, and that's the way *I* always have felt about *mine*. But your dad looks like a great guy to me, so—well, maybe mine could be too, if I gave him a chance. Your dad was saying I should."

"Should what? You should go home?"

"No. Your dad said I ought to write him a long letter and face up to all the things I've goofed on. Quitting NYU, the cellar trouble, all that. Then tell him I'm going to get a job and go to night school. Your dad figures probably he'd help me. He said he'd write him, too. No reason he should. I'm nothing in his life. It's pretty nice of him."

I try to digest all this, and it sure is puzzling. The time I ran down that crumb of a doorman on my bike, accidental on purpose, I didn't get any long understanding talks. I just got kept in for a month.

Tom slaps me in the middle of the back and stands up. "Hilda's gone back to work at the coffee shop. I guess I'll go down and see her before the lunch rush, and then go home and write my letter."

"Say 'Hi' for me."

"O.K. So long."

The weather cools off some, and Pop starts to talk about vacation. He's taking two weeks, last of August and first of September, so I start shopping

around for various bits of fishing tackle and picnic gear we might need. We're going to this lake
up in Connecticut, where we get a sort of motel
cottage. It has a little hot plate for making coffee
in the morning, but most of the rest of the time we
eat out, which is neat.

We're sitting around the living room one evening, sorting stuff out, when the doorbell rings. I go
answer it, and Tom walks in. He nods at me like
he hardly sees me and comes into the living room.
He shakes hands like a wooden Indian. His face
looks shut up again, the way it did that day I left
him in the filling station.

He reaches in his pocket and pulls out a letter.
I can see a post-office stamp in red ink with a
pointing hand by the address. He throws it down
on Dad's table.

"I got my answer all right."

Pop looks at the letter and I see his foot start to
twitch the way it does when he's about to blow.
But he looks at Tom, and instead of blowing he
just says, "Your father left town? No forwarding
address?"

"I guess so. He just left. Him and that woman
he married." Tom's voice trails off and he walks
over to the window. We all sit quiet a minute.

Finally Pop says gently, "Well, don't waste too much breath on her. She's nothing to do with you."

Tom turns around angrily. "She's no good. She loafs around and drinks all the time. She talked him into going."

"And he went." There's another short silence, and Pop goes on. "Where was this you lived?"

"House. It was a pretty nice little house, too. Dark red with white trim, and enough of a yard to play a little ball, and I grew a few lettuces every spring. I even got one ear of corn once. We moved there when I was in second grade because my mom said it was near a good local school. I lived there till I went to college. I suppose he sold it, or got a loan, and they lit off to drink it up. Soon's they'd got *me* off their hands."

Tom bites off the last word. Suddenly I can see the picture pretty clear: the nice house, the father Tom always talked down and hoped would measure up. Now it's like somebody has taken his whole childhood and crumpled it up like a wad of tissue paper and thrown it away.

Mom gets up and goes into the kitchen. Pop's foot keeps on twitching. Finally he says, "Well, I steered you wrong. I'm sorry. But maybe it's just as well to have it settled."

"It's settled, all right," Tom says.

Mom brings out a tray of ginger-ale glasses. It seems sort of inadequate at a moment like this, but when Tom takes a glass from her he looks like he's going to bust out crying.

He drinks some and blows his nose, and Dad says, "When are you supposed to check in with the Youth Board again?"

"Tuesday. My day off. And I wind up the filling-station job the next week, right after Labor Day."

"Labor Day. Hm-m. We've got to get moving. If you like, I'll come down to the Youth Board with you, and we'll see what we can all cook up. Don't worry too much. I have a feeling you're just beginning to fight—really fight, not just throw a few stones."

"I don't know why you bother." Tom starts to stand up. But while we've been talking, Cat has been creeping up under the side table, playing the ambush game, and he launches himself at Tom just as he starts to stand. It throws him off balance and he sits back in the chair, holding Cat.

"You've got nothing to worry about," Pop says. "Cat's on your side."

10

CAT AND THE PARKWAY

Cat may be on Tom's side, but whether Pop is on Cat's side is something else again. I worry about this all the time we're planning the vacation. Suppose the motel won't take cats? Or suppose he runs away in the country? If he messes up the vacation in any way, I know Pop'll say to get rid of him.

I practice putting Cat back in the wicker hamper to see if I can keep him in that sometimes, but he meows like crazy. That'd drive Pop nuts in the car, and it certainly wouldn't hide him from any motel-keeper. So I just sit back and hope for the best, but I got a nasty feeling in the bottom of my stomach that some thing's going to go haywire.

Pop's pretty snappish anyway. He's working late nearly every night, getting stuff cleared up before vacation. He doesn't want any extra problems, especially not Cat problems. Mom's been having asthma a good deal lately, and we're all pretty jumpy. It's always like this at the end of the summer.

Tuesday night when he gets home, I ask Pop what's happened about Tom.

"We'll work something out," he says, which isn't what you'd call a big explanation.

"You think he can get back into college?"

"I don't know. The Youth Board is going to work on it. They're arranging for him to make up the midyear exams he missed, so he can get credit for that semester. Then he can probably start making up the second semester at night school if he has a job.

"Apparently the Youth Board knew his father had skipped—they've been trying to trace him. I don't think it'll do any good if they find him. Tom had better just cross him off and figure his own life for himself."

You know, I see "bad guys" in television and stuff, but with the people I really know I always lump the parents on one team and the kids on the other. Now here's my pop calmly figuring a kid better chalk off his father as a bad lot and go it alone. If your father died, I suppose you could face up to it eventually, but having him just fade out on you, not care what you did—that'd be worse.

While I'm doing all this hard thinking, Pop has gone back to reading the paper. I notice the column of want ads on the back, and all of a sudden my mind clicks on Tom and jobs.

"Hey, Pop! You know the florist on the corner, Palumbo, where you always get Mom the plant on Mother's Day? I went in there a couple of weeks ago, because he had a sign up, 'Helper Wanted.' I thought maybe it was deliveries and stuff that I could do after school. But he said he needed a full-time man. I'm pretty sure the sign's still up."

"Palumbo, huhn?" Pop takes off his glasses and scratches his head with them. He looks at his watch and sighs. "They still open?"

They are, and Pop goes right down to see the guy. He knows him fairly well anyway—there's

Mother's Day, and Easter, and also the shop is the polling place for our district, so Pop's in there every Election Day. He always buys some little bunch of flowers Election Day because he figures the guy ought to get some business having his shop all messed up for the day.

Dad comes back and goes over to the desk and scratches off a fast note. He says, "Here. Address it to Tom and go mail it right away. Palumbo says he'll try him out at least. Tom can come over Thursday night and I'll take him in."

Tom comes home with Pop Thursday about nine o'clock. They both look pretty good. Mom has cold supper waiting, finishing off the icebox before we go away, so we all sit down to eat.

"Tom's all set, at least for a start," Dad says. "He's going to start Tuesday, right after Labor Day. Palumbo can use him on odd jobs and deliveries, especially over the Jewish holidays, and then if he can learn the business, he'll keep him on."

"Never thought I'd go in for flower-arranging." Tom grins. "But it might be fun. I'm pretty fair at any kind of handiwork."

Remembering how quick he unlocked the padlock to get Cat out in the cellar, I agree.

He starts for his room after supper, and we all

say "good luck," "have a good time," and stuff. Things are really looking up.

I get up early the next morning and help Mom button up around the house and get the car loaded before Pop gets home in the afternoon. He hoped to get off early, and I've been pacing around snapping my fingers for a couple of hours when he finally arrives about six o'clock. It's a hot day again.

I don't say anything about Cat. I just dive in the back seat and put him behind a suitcase and hope he'll behave. Pop doesn't seem to notice him. Anyway he doesn't say anything.

It's mighty hot, and traffic is thick, with everyone pouring out of the city. But at least we're moving along, until we get out on the Hutchinson River Parkway, where some dope has to run out of gas.

All three lanes of traffic are stopped. We sit in the sun. Pop looks around, hunting for something to get sore about, and sees the back windows are closed. He roars, "Crying out loud, can't we get some air, at least? Open those windows!"

I open them and try to keep my hand over Cat, but if you try to hold him really, it makes him restless. For the moment he's sitting quiet, looking disgusted.

We sit for about ten minutes, and Pop turns off the motor. You can practically hear us sweating in the silence. Engines turn on ahead of us, and there seems to be some sign of hope. I stick my head out the window to see if things are moving. Something furry tickles my ear, and it takes me a second to register.

Then I grab, but too late. There is Cat, out on the parkway between the lanes of cars, trying to figure which way to run.

"Pop!" I yell. "Hold it! Cat's got out!"

You know what my pop does? He laughs.

"Hold it, my eyeball!" he says. "I've been holding it for half an hour. I'd get murdered if I tried to stop now. Besides, I don't want to chase that cat every day of my vacation."

I don't even stop to think. I just open the car door and jump. The car's only barely moving. I can see Cat on the grass at the edge of the parkway. The cars in the next lane blast their horns, but I slip through and grab Cat.

I hear Mom scream, "Davey!"

Our car is twenty feet ahead, now, in the center lane, and there's no way Pop can turn off. The cars are picking up speed. I holler to Mom as loud as I can, "I'll go back and stay with Kate! Don't worry!"

I hear Pop shout about something, but I can't hear what. Pretty soon the car is out of sight. I look down at Cat and say, "There goes our vacation." I wonder if I'll be able to catch a bus out to Connecticut later. Meanwhile, there's the little problem of getting back into the city. I'm standing alongside the parkway, with railroad tracks and the Pelham golf course on the other side of me, and a good long walk to the subway.

A cat isn't handy to walk with. He keeps trying to get down. If you squeeze him to hang on, he just tries harder. You have to keep juggling him, like, gently. I sweat along back, with the sun in my eyes, and people in cars on the parkway pointing me out to their children as a local curiosity.

One place the bulrushes and marsh grass beside the road grow up higher than your head. What a place for a kids' hideout, I think. Almost the next step, I hear kids' voices, whispering and shushing each other.

Their voices follow along beside me, but inside the curtain of rushes, where I can't see them. I hear one say, "Lookit the sissy with the kitty!" Another answers, "Let's dump 'em in the river!"

I try to walk faster, but I figure if I run they'll

chase me for sure. I walk along, juggling Cat, trying to pretend I don't notice them. I see a drawbridge up ahead, and I sure hope there's a cop or watchman on it.

The kids break out of the rushes behind me, and there's no use pretending anymore. I flash a look over my shoulder. They all yell, "Ya-n-h-h-h!" like a bunch of wild Indians, but they're about fifty feet back.

I grab Cat hard about the only place you can grab a cat, around one upper forearm, and I really run. The kids let out another war whoop. It's uphill to the bridge. Cat gets his free forepaw into action, raking my chest and arm, with his claws out. Then he hisses and bites, and I nearly drop him. I'm panting so hard I can't hardly breathe anyway.

A cop saunters out on my approach to the bridge, his billy dangling from his wrist. Whew—am I glad! I flop on the grass and ease up on Cat and start soothing him down. The kids fade off into the tall grass as soon as they see the cop. A stone arches up toward me, but it falls short. That's the last I see of them.

As I cross the bridge, the cop squints at me. "What you doing, kid? Not supposed to be walking here."

"I'll be right off. I'm going home," I tell him, and he saunters away, twirling his stick.

It's dark by the time I get to the subway, and most of another hour before I'm back in Manhattan and reach Kate's. I can hear the television going, which is unusual, and I walk in. No one is watching television. Mom and Pop are sitting at the table with Kate.

Mom lets loose the tears she has apparently been holding onto for two hours, and Pop starts bellowing: "You fool! You might have got killed jumping out on that parkway!"

Cat drops to the floor with a thud. I kiss Mom and go to the sink for a long glass of water and drink it all and wipe my mouth. Over my shoulder, I answer Pop: "Yeah, but if Cat gets killed on the parkway, that's just a big joke, isn't it? You laugh your head off!"

Pop takes off his glasses and scratches his head with them, like he always does when he's thinking. He looks me in the eye and says, "I'm sorry. I shouldn't have laughed."

Then, of all things, he picks up Cat himself. "Come on. You're one of the family. Let's get on this vacation."

At last we're off.

11

ROSH HASHANAH AT THE FULTON FISH MARKET

We came back to the city Labor Day Monday—us and a couple million others—traffic crawling, a hot day, the windows practically closed up tight to keep Cat in. I sweated, and then cat hairs stuck to me and got up my nose. Considering every-thing, Pop acted quite mild.

I met a kid up at the lake in Connecticut who had skin-diving equipment. He let me use it one day when Mom and Pop were off sightseeing. Boy, this has fishing beat hollow! I found out there's a skin-diving course at the Y, and I'm going to begin saving up for the fins and mask and stuff. Pop won't mind forking out for the Y membership, because he'll figure it's character-building.

Meanwhile, I'm wondering if I can get back up to Connecticut again one weekend while the weather's still warm, and I see that Rosh Hashanah falls on a Monday and Tuesday this year, the week after school opens. Great. So I ask this kid— Kenny Wright—if I can maybe come visit him that weekend so I can do some more skin diving.

"Rosh Hashanah? What's that?" he says.

So I explain to him. Rosh Hashanah is the Jewish New Year. About half the kids in my school are Jewish, so they all stay out for it, and I always do too. Last year the school board gave up and made it an official school holiday for everyone, Jewish or not. Same with Yom Kippur, the week after.

Kenny whistles. "You sure are lucky. I don't think we got any holidays coming till Thanksgiving."

I always thought the kids in the country were lucky having outdoor yards for sports and recess, but I guess we have it over them on holidays— 'specially in the fall: three Jewish holidays in September, Columbus Day in October, Election Day and Veterans' Day in November, and then

Thanksgiving. It drives the mothers wild.

I don't figure it'd be worth train fare to Connecticut for just two days, so I say good-bye to Kenny and see you next year and stuff.

Back home I'm pretty busy right away, on account of starting in a new school, Charles Evans Hughes High. It's different from the junior high, where I knew half the kids, and also my whole homeroom there went from one classroom to another together. At Hughes everyone has to get his own schedule and find the right classroom in this immense building, which is about the size of Penn Station. There are about a million kids in it—actually about two thousand—most of whom I never saw before. Hardly any of the Stuyvesant Town and Peter Cooper Village kids come here because it isn't their district. However, walking back across Fifth Avenue one day, I see one kid I know from Peter Cooper. His name is Ben Alstein. I ask him how come he is at Hughes.

"My dad wanted me to get into Peter Stuyvesant High School—you know, the genius factory, city-wide competitive exam to get in. Of course I didn't make it. Biggest Failure of the Year, that's me."

"Heck, I never even tried for that. But how come you're here?"

"There's a special science course you can qualify for by taking a math test. Then you don't have to live in the district. My dad figures as long as I'm in something special, there's hope. I'm not really very interested in science, but that doesn't bother him."

So after that Ben and I walk back and forth to school together, and it turns out we have three classes together, too—biology and algebra and English. We're both relieved to have at least one familiar face to look for in the crowd. My old friend Nick, aside from not really being my best friend anymore, has gone to a Catholic high school somewhere uptown.

On the way home from school one Friday in September, I ask Ben what he's doing Monday and Tuesday, the Jewish holidays.

"Tuesday I got to get into my bar mitzvah suit and go to synagogue and over to Brooklyn to my grandmother's. Monday I don't have to do anything special. Come on over with your roller skates and we'll get in the hockey game.'

"I skate on my tail," I say, because it's true, and it would be doubly true in a hockey game. I try quick to think up something else. We're walking down the block to my house, and there's Cat

sitting out front, so I say, "Let's cruise around
and get down to Fulton Fish Market and pick up
some fish heads for my cat."

"You're a real nut, aren't you?" Ben says. He
doesn't say it as if he minds—just mentioning
the fact. He's an easygoing kind of guy, and I
think most of the time he likes to let someone
else make the plans. So he shrugs and says,
"O.K."

I introduce him to Cat. Ben looks him in the eye,
and Cat looks away and licks his back. Ben says,
"So I got to get you fresh fish for Rosh Hashanah,
huh?"

Cat jumps down and rubs from back to front
against Ben's right leg and from front to back
against his left leg and goes to lie down in the
middle of the sidewalk.

"See? He likes you," I say. "He won't have anything to do with most guys, except Tom."

"Who's Tom?"

So I tell Ben all about Tom and the cellar and
his father disappearing on him.

"Gee," says Ben, "I thought I had trouble, with
my father practically telling me how to breathe
better every minute, but at least he doesn't disappear. What does Tom do now?"

"Works at the flower shop, right down there at the corner."

Ben feels around in his pockets a minute. "Hey, I got two bucks I was supposed to spend on a textbook. Come on and I'll buy Mom a plant for the holidays, and you can introduce me to Tom."

We go down to the flower shop, and at first Tom frowns because he thinks we've just come to kid around. Ben tells him he wants a plant, so then he makes a big thing out of showing him all the plants, from the ten-dollar ones on down, so Mr. Palumbo will see he's doing a good job. Ben finally settles on a funny-looking cactus that Tom says is going to bloom pretty soon.

Ben goes along home and I arrange to pick him up on Monday. I wait around outside until I see Tom go out on a delivery and ask him how he likes the job. He says he doesn't really know yet, but at least the guy is decent to work for, not like the filling-station man.

I sleep late Monday and go over to Peter Cooper about eleven. A lot of kids are out in the playgrounds, and some fathers are there tossing footballs with them and shouting "Happy New Year" to each other. It sounds odd to hear people saying that on a warm day in September.

Ben and I wander out of the project and he says, "How do we get to this Fulton Street?"

I see a bus that says "Avenue C" on it stopping on Twenty-third Street. Avenue C is way east, and so is Fulton Street, so I figure it'll probably work out. We get on. The bus rockets along under the East Side Drive for a few blocks and then heads down Avenue C, which is narrow and crowded. It's a Spanish and Puerto Rican neighborhood to begin with, then farther downtown it's mostly Jewish. Lots of people are out on the street shaking hands and clapping each other on the back, and the stores are all closed.

Every time the bus stops, the driver shouts to some of the people on the sidewalk, and he seems to know a good many of the passengers who get on. He asks them about their jobs, or their babies, or their aunt who's sick in Bellevue. This is pretty unusual in New York, where bus drivers usually act like they hate people in general and their passengers in particular. Suddenly the bus turns off Avenue C and heads west.

Ben looks out the window and says, "Hey, this is Houston Street. I been down here to a big delicatessen. But we're not heading downtown anymore."

"Probably it'll turn again," I say.

It doesn't, though, not till clear over at Sixth Avenue. By then everyone else has got off and the bus driver turns around and says, "Where you two headed for?"

It's funny, a bus driver asking you that, so I ask him, "Where does this bus go?"

"It goes from Bellevue Hospital down to Hudson Street, down by the Holland Tunnel."

"Holy cow!" says Ben. "We're liable to wind up in New Jersey."

"Relax. I don't go that far. I just go back up to Bellevue," says the driver.

"You think we'd be far from Fulton Fish Market?" I say.

The driver gestures vaguely. "Just across the island."

So Ben and I decide we'll get off at the end of the line and walk from there. The bus driver says, "Have a nice hike."

"I think there's something fishy about this," says Ben.

"That's what we're going to get, fish," I say, and we walk. We walk quite a ways.

Ben sees a little Italian restaurant down a couple of steps, and we stop to look at the menu in the window. The special for the day is lasagna, and Ben says, "Boy, that's for me!"

We go inside, while I finger the dollar in my pocket and do some fast mental arithmetic. Lasagna is a dollar, so that's out, but I see spaghetti and meat balls is seventy-five cents, so that will still leave me bus fare home.

A waiter rushes up, wearing a white napkin over his arm like a banner, and takes our order. He returns in a moment with a shiny clean white linen tablecloth and a basket of fresh Italian bread and rolls. On a third trip he brings enough chilled butter for a family and asks if we want coffee with lunch or later. Later, we say.

"Man, this is living!" says Ben as he moves in on the bread.

"He treats us just like people."

Pretty soon the waiter is back with our lasagna and spaghetti, and he swirls around the table as if he were dancing. "Anything else now? Mind the hot plates, very hot! Have a good lunch now. I bring the coffee later."

He swirls away, the napkin over his arm making a little breeze, and circles another table. It's a small room, and there are only four tables eating, but he seems to enjoy acting like he was serving royalty at the Waldorf. When we're just finished eating, he comes back with a pot of steaming coffee and a pitcher of real cream.

I'm dolloping the cream in, and it floats, when a thought hits me: We got to leave a tip for this waiter.

I whisper to Ben, "Hey, how much money you got?"

He reaches in his pocket and fishes out a buck, a dime, and a quarter. We study them. Figure coffees for a dime each, and the total check ought to be $1.95. We've got $2.35 between us. We can still squeak through with bus fare if we only leave the waiter a dime, which is pretty cheap.

At that moment he comes back and refills our coffee cups and asks what we will have for dessert.

"Uh, nothing, nothing at all," I say.

"Couldn't eat another thing," says Ben.

So the waiter brings the check and along with it a plate of homemade cookies. He says, "My wife make. On the house."

We both thank him, and I look at Ben and he looks at me. I put down my dollar and he puts down a dollar and a quarter.

"Thank you, gentlemen, thank you. Come again," says the waiter.

We walk into the street, and Ben spins the lone

remaining dime in the sun. I say, "Heads or tails?"

"Huh? Heads."

It comes up heads, so Ben keeps his own dime. He says, "We could have hung onto enough for *one* bus fare, but that's no use."

"No use at all. 'Specially if it was yours."

"Are we still heading for Fulton Street?"

"Sure. We got to get fish for Cat."

"It better be for free."

We walk, threading across Manhattan and downtown. I guess it's thirty or forty blocks, but after a good lunch it doesn't seem too far.

You can smell the fish market when you're still quite a ways off. It runs for a half a dozen blocks alongside the East River, with long rows of sheds divided into stores for the different wholesalers. Around on the side streets there are bars and fish restaurants. It's too bad we don't have Cat with us because he'd love sniffing at all the fish heads and guts and stuff on the street. Fish market business is done mostly in the morning, I guess, and now men are hosing down the streets and sweeping fish garbage up into piles. I get a guy to give me a bag and select a couple of the choicer—and cleaner—looking bits. I get a nice red snapper head and a small whole fish, looks like a mackerel. Ben acts as if fish guts make him sick, and as soon as I've got a couple he starts saying "Come on, come on, let's go."

I realize when we're leaving that I don't even notice the fish smell anymore. You just get used to it. We walk uptown, quite a hike, along East Broadway and across Grand and Delancey. There's all kinds of intriguing smells wafting around here: hot breads and pickles and fish cooking. This is a real Jewish neighborhood, and you can sure tell it's a holiday from the smell of all the dinners cooking. And lots of people are out in their best clothes gabbing together. Some of the men wear black skullcaps, and some of them have big black felt hats and long white beards. We go past a crowd gathering outside a movie house.

"They're not going to the movies," Ben says. "On holidays sometimes they rent a movie theater for services. It must be getting near time. Come on, I got to hurry."

We trot along the next twenty blocks or so, up First Avenue and to Peter Cooper.

"So long," Ben says. "I'll come by Wednesday on the way to school."

He goes off spinning his dime, and too late I think to myself that we could have had a candy bar.

12
THE RED EFT

Ben and I both take biology, and the first weekend assignment we get, right after Rosh Hashanah, is to find and identify an animal native to New York City and look up its family and species and life cycle.

"What's a species?" says Ben.

"I don't know. What's a life cycle?"

We both scratch our heads, and he says, "What animals do we know?"

I say, "Cat. And dogs and pigeons and squirrels."

"That's dull. I want to get some animal no one else knows about."

"Hey, how about a praying mantis? I saw one once in Gramercy Park."

Ben doesn't even know what it is, so I tell him about this one I saw. For an insect, it looks almost like a dragon, about four or five inches long and pale green. When it flies, it looks like a baby helicopter in the sky. We go into Gramercy Park to see if we can find another, but we can't.

Ben says, "Let's go up to the Bronx Zoo Saturday and see what we can find."

"Stupid, they don't mean you to do lions and tigers. They're not native."

"Stupid, yourself. They got other animals that are. Besides, there's lots of woods and ponds. I might find something."

Well, it's as good an idea for Saturday as any, so I say O.K. On account of both being pretty broke, we take lunch along in my old school lunchbox. Also six subway tokens—two extras for emergencies. Even I would be against walking home from the Bronx.

Of course there are plenty of native New York City animals in the zoo—raccoons and woodchucks and moles and lots of birds—and I figure we better start home not too late to get out the encyclopedias for species and life cycles. Ben still wants to catch something wild and wonderful. Like lots of city kids who haven't been in the country much, he's crazy about nature.

We head back to the subway, walking through the woods so he can hunt. We go down alongside the pond and kick up rocks and dead trees to see if anything is under them.

It pays off. All of a sudden we see a tiny red tail disappearing under a rotten log. I push the log again and Ben grabs. It's a tiny lizard, not more than two or three inches long and brick red all over. Ben cups it in both hands, and its throat pulses in and out, but it doesn't really try to get away.

"Hey, I love this one!" Ben cries. "I'm going to take him home and keep him for a pet, as well as do a report on him. You can't keep cats and dogs in Peter Cooper, but there's nothing in the rules about lizards."

"How are you going to get him home?"

"Dump the lunch. I mean—we'll eat it, but I can stab a hole in the top of the box and keep Redskin in it. Come on, hurry! He's getting tired in my hand I think!"

Ben is one of those guys who is very placid most of the time, but he gets excitable all of a sudden when he runs into something brand-new to him, and I guess he never caught an animal to keep before. Some people's parents are very stuffy about it.

I dump the lunch out, and he puts the lizard in and selects some particular leaves and bits of dead log to put in with him to make him feel at home. Without even asking me, he takes out his knife and makes holes in the top of my lunchbox. I sit down and open up a sandwich, but Ben is still dancing around.

"What do you suppose he is? He might be something very rare! How'm I going to find out? You think we ought to go back and ask one of the zoo men?"

"Umm, nah," I say, chewing. "Probably find him in the encyclopedia."

Ben squats on a log, and the log rolls. As he falls over backward I see two more lizards scuttle away. I grab one. "Hey, look! I got another. This one's bigger and browner."

Ben is up and dancing again. "Oh, boy, oh, boy! Now I got two! Now they'll be happy! Maybe they'll have babies, huh?"

He overlooks the fact that *I* caught this one. Oh, well, I don't want a lizard, anyway. Cat'd probably eat it.

Ben takes it from me and slips it in the lunchbox. "I'm going to call this one Big Brownie."

Finally he calms down enough to eat lunch, taking peeks at his catch between mouthfuls. As soon as he's finished eating, he starts hustling to get home so he can make a house for them. He really acts like a kid.

We get on the subway. It's aboveground—elevated—up here in the Bronx. After a while I see Yankee Stadium off to one side, which is funny because I don't remember seeing it when we were coming up. Pretty soon the train goes underground. I remember then. Coming up, we changed trains once. Ben has his eye glued to the edge of the lunchbox and he's talking to Redskin, so I figure there's no use consulting him. I'll just wait and see where this train seems to come out. It's got to go downtown. We go past something called Lenox Avenue, which I think is in Harlem, then Ninety-sixth Street, and then we're at Columbus Circle.

"Hey, Ben, we're on the West Side subway," I say.

"Yeah?" He takes a bored look out the window.
"We can just walk across town from Fourteenth
Street."

"With you I always end up walking. Hey, what
about those extra tokens?"

"Aw, it's only a few blocks. Let's walk."

Ben grunts, and he goes along with me. As we
get near Union Square, there seem to be an awful
lot of people around. In fact they're jamming the
sidewalk and we can hardly move. Ben frowns at
them and says, "Hey, what goes?"

I ask a man, and he says, "Where you been,
sonny? Don'tcha know there's a parade for General Sparks?"

I remember reading about it now, so I poke Ben.
"Hey, push along! We can see Sparks go by!"

"Quit pushing and don't try to be funny."

"Stupid, he's a general. Test pilot, war hero, and
stuff. Come on, push."

"QUIT PUSHING! I got to watch out for these
lizards!"

So I go first and edge us through the crowd to
the middle of the block, where there aren't so
many people and we can get up next to the police
barrier. Cops on horseback are going back and
forth, keeping the street clear. No sign of any

parade coming yet, but people are throwing rolls of paper tape and handfuls of confetti out of upper-story windows. The wind catches the paper tape and carries it up and around in all kinds of fantastic snakes. Little kids keep scuttling under the barrier to grab handfuls of ticker tape that blow to the ground. Ben keeps one eye on the street and one on Redskin and Brownie.

"How soon you think they're coming?" he asks fretfully.

People have packed in behind us, and we couldn't leave now if we wanted to. Pretty soon we can see a helicopter flying low just a little ways downtown, and people all start yelling, "That's where they are! They're coming!"

Suddenly a bunch of motorcycle cops zoom past, and then a cop backing up a police car at about thirty miles an hour, which is a very surprising-looking thing. Before I've hardly got my eyes off that, the open cars come by. This guy Sparks is sitting up on the back of the car, waving with both hands. By the time I see him, he's almost past. Nice-looking, though. Everyone yells like crazy and throws any kind of paper they've got. Two little nuts beside us have a box of Wheaties, so they're busy throwing Breakfast of Champions. As soon as the motorcade is past, people push through the barriers and run in the street.

Ben hunches over to protect his precious animals and yells, "Come on! Let's get out of this!"

We go into my house first because I'm pretty sure we've got a wooden box. We find it and take it down to my room, and Ben gets extra leaves and grass and turns the lizards into it. He's sure they need lots of fresh air and exercise. Redskin scoots out of sight into a corner right away. Big Brownie sits by a leaf and looks around.

"Let's go look up what they are," I say.

The smallest lizard they show in the encyclopedia is about six inches long, and it says lizards are reptiles and have scales and claws and should not be confused with salamanders, which are amphibians and have thin moist skin and no claws. So we look up salamanders.

This is it, all right. The first picture on the page looks just like Redskin, and it says he's a Red Eft. The Latin name for his species is *Triturus viridescens,* or in English just a common newt.

"Hey, talk about life cycles, listen to this," says Ben, reading. " 'It hatches from an egg in the water and stays there during its first summer as a dull-green larva. Then its skin becomes a bright orange, it absorbs its gills, develops lungs and legs, and crawls out to live for about three years in the woods. When fully mature, its back turns dull again, and it returns to the water to breed.'"

Ben drops the book. "Brownie must be getting ready to breed! What'd I tell you? We got to put him near water!" He rushes down to my room.

We come to the door and stop short. There's Cat, poised on the edge of the box.

I grab, but no kid is as fast as a cat. Hearing me coming, he makes his grab for the salamander. Then he's out of the box and away, with Big Brownie's tail hanging out of his mouth. He goes under the bed.

Ben screams, "Get him! Kill him! He's got my Brownie!" He's in a frenzy, and I don't blame him. It does make you mad to see your pet get hurt. I run for a broom to try to poke Cat out, but it isn't any use. Meanwhile, Ben finds Redskin safe in the box, and he scoops him back into the lunchbox.

Finally, we move the bed, and there is Cat poking daintily with his paw at Brownie. The salamander is dead. Ben grabs the broom and bashes Cat. Cat hisses and skids down the hall. "That rotten cat! I wish I could kill him! What'd you ever have him for?"

I tell Ben I'm sorry, and I get him a little box so he can bury Brownie. You can't really blame Cat too much—that's just the way a cat is made, to chase anything that wiggles and runs. Ben calms down after a while, and we go back to the encyclopedia to finish looking up about the Red Eft.

"I don't think Brownie was really ready to lay eggs, or he would have been in the pond already," I say. "Tell you what. We could go back some day with a jar and try to catch one in the water."

That cheers Ben up some. He finishes taking notes for his report and tracing a picture, and then he goes home with Redskin in the lunchbox. I pull out the volume for C.

Cat. Family, *Felidae*, including lions and tigers. Species, *Felis domesticus*. I start taking notes: " 'The first civilized people to keep cats were the Egyptians, thirteen centuries before Christ. . . . Fifty million years earlier the ancestor of the cat family roamed the earth, and he is the ancestor of all present-day carnivores. The Oligocene cats, thirty million years ago, were already highly specialized, and the habits and physical characteristics of cats have been fixed since then. This may explain why house cats remain the most independent of pets, with many of the instincts of their wild ancestors.' "

I call Ben up to read him this, and he says, "You and your lousy carnivore! *My* salamander is an amphibian, and amphibians are the ancestors of *all* the animals on earth, even you and your Cat, you sons of toads!"

13

THE LEFT BANK OF CONEY ISLAND

Columbus Day comes up as cold as Christmas. I listen to the weather forecast the night before, to see how it'll be for the beach. "High winds, unseasonably low temperatures," the guy says. He would.

I get up at eight-thirty the next morning, though, figuring he'd be wrong and it would be a nice sunny day. I slip on my pants and shirt and go downstairs with Cat to have a look out. Cat slides out and is halfway down the stoop when a blast of cold wind hits him. His tail goes up and he spooks back in between my legs. I push the door shut against the icy wind.

Mom is sitting in the kitchen drinking her tea and she says, "My goodness, why are you up so early on a holiday? Do you feel sick?"

"Nah, I'm all right." I pour out a cup of coffee to warm my hands on and dump in three or four spoons of sugar.

"Davey, have you got a chill? You don't look to me as if you felt quite right."

"Mom, for Pete's sake, it's COLD out! I feel fine."

"Well, you don't have to go out. Why don't you just go back to bed and snooze and read a bit, and I'll bring you some breakfast."

I see it's got to be faced, so while I'm getting down the cereal and a bowl, I say, "Well, as a matter of fact, I'm going over to Coney Island today."

"Coney ISLAND!" Mom sounds like it was Siberia. "What in the world are you going to do there in the middle of winter?"

"Mom, it's only Columbus Day. We figured we'd go to the aquarium and then—uh—well, fool around. Some of the pitches are still open, and we'll get hot dogs and stuff."

"Who's going? Nick?"

"Nick wasn't sure—I'll stop by his house and

see." I'd just as soon steer clear of this "who's going" business, so I start into a long spiel about how we're studying marine life in biology, and we have to take some notes at the aquarium. Mom is swallowing this pretty well, but Pop comes into the kitchen just then and gives me the fishy eye.

"First time I ever heard of you spending a holiday on homework. I bet they got a new twist palace going out there."

I slam down my coffee cup. "Holy cats! Can't I walk out of here on a holiday without going through the third degree? What am I, some kind of a nut or a convict?"

"Just a growing boy," says Pop. "And don't talk so sassy to your mother."

"I'm talking to you!"

Pop draws in a breath to start bellowing, but Mom beats him to it by starting to wheeze, which she can do without drawing breath.

Pop pats her on the shoulder and gives me a dirty look. "Now, Agnes, that's all right. I'm not sore. I was just trying to kid him a little bit, and he flies off the handle."

I fly off the handle! How do you like that?

I give Mom a kiss. "Cheer up, Mom. I won't ride on the roller coaster. It's not even running."

I grab a sweater and gloves and money and get out before they can start anymore questions. On the subway I start wondering if Mary will show up. It's almost two months since we made this sort of crazy date, and the weather sure isn't helping any.

Coney Island is made to be crowded and noisy. All the billboards scream at you, as if they had to get your attention. So when the place is empty, it looks like the whole thing was a freak or an accident.

It's sure empty today. There's practically no one on the street in the five or six blocks from the subway station to the aquarium. But it's not quiet. There are a few places open—merry-go-rounds and hot-dog shops—and tinny little trickles of music come out of them, but the big noise is the wind. All the signs are swinging and screeching. Rubbish cans blow over and their tops clang and bang rolling down the street. The wind makes a whistling noise all by itself.

I lean into the wind and walk up the empty street. My sweater is about as warm as a sieve. I wonder if I'm crazy to have come. No girl would get out on a boardwalk on a day like this. It must be practically a hurricane.

She's there, though. As soon as I turn the corner to the beach, I can see one figure, with its back to the ocean, scarf and hair blowing inland toward me. I can't see her face, but it's Mary, all right. There isn't another soul in sight. I wave and she hunches her shoulders up and down to semaphore, not wishing to take her hands out of her pockets.

I come up beside her on the boardwalk and turn my back to the ocean, too. I'd like to go on looking at it—it's all black and white and thundery—but the wind blows your breath right back down into your stomach. I freeze.

"I was afraid you wouldn't come on a day like this," I say.

"Me too. I mean I was afraid *you* wouldn't."

"Mom and Pop thought I was crazy. I spent about an hour arguing with them. What'd your mother say?"

"Nothing. She thinks I'm walking alone with the wind in my hair, thinking poetic thoughts."

"Huh? What for?"

Mary shrugs. "Mom's like that. You'll see. Come on, let's go home and make cocoa or something to warm up, and then we'll think up something to do. We can't just stand here."

She's right about that, so I don't argue. Her house is a few blocks away, a two-family type with a sloped driveway going down into a cellar garage. Neat. My pop is always going nuts hunting for a place to park.

Mary goes in and shouts, "Hi, Nina! I brought a friend home. We're going to make some cocoa. We're freezing."

I wonder who Nina is. I don't hear her mother come into the kitchen. Then I turn around and there she is. Holy cow! We got some pretty beat-looking types at school, but this is the first time I've ever seen a beatnik mother.

She's got on a black T-shirt and blue jeans and old sneakers, and her hair is in a long braid, with uneven bangs in front.

Mary waves a saucepan vaguely at us both and says, "Nina—Davey—this is my mother."

So Nina is her mother. I stick out my hand. "Uh—how do you do?"

"Hel-looo." Her voice is low and musical. "I think there is coffee on the stove."

"I thought I'd make cocoa for a change," says Mary.

"All right." Nina puts a cigarette in her mouth and offers one to me.

I say, "No, thank you."

"Tell me . . ." She talks in this low, intense kind of voice. "Are you in school with Mary?"

So I tell her I live in Manhattan, and how I ran into Mary when I had Cat on the beach, because that makes it sound sort of respectable, not like a pickup. But she doesn't seem to be interested in Cat and the beach.

"What do you *read?* In your school?" she asks, launching each question like a torpedo.

I remember Mary saying something about her mother and poetry, so I say, "Well, uh—last week we read 'The Highwayman' and 'The Wreck of the Hesperus.' They're about—I mean, we were studying metaphors and similes. Looking at the ocean today, I sure can see what Longfellow meant about the icy . . ."

I thought I was doing pretty well, but she cut me off again.

"Don't you read any *real* poetry? Donne? Auden? Baudelaire?"

Three more torpedoes. "We didn't get to them yet."

Nina blows out a great angry cloud of smoke and explodes, "Schools!" Then she sails out of the kitchen.

I guess I look a little shook up. Mary laughs and shoves a mug of cocoa and a plate of cinnamon toast in front of me. "Don't mind Mother. She just can't get used to New York schools. Or Coney Island. Or hardly anything around here.

"She grew up on the Left Bank in Paris. Her father was an artist and her mother was a writer, and they taught her to read at home, starting with Chaucer, probably. She never read a kids' book in her life.

"Anything I ever tell her about school pretty much sounds either childish or stupid to her. What I really love is science—experiments and stuff—and she can't see that for beans."

"Our science teacher is a dope," I say, because she is, "so I really never got very interested in science. But I told Mom and Dad I was coming to the aquarium to take notes today, so they wouldn't kick up such a fuss."

Mary shakes her head. "We ought to get our mothers together. Mine thinks I'm wasting time if I even *go* to the aquarium. I do, though, all the time. I love the walrus."

"What does your pop do?"

"Father? He teaches philosophy at Brooklyn College. So I get it from both sides. Just think,

think, think. Father and Nina aren't hardly even interested in *food*. Once in a while Nina spends all day cooking some great fish soup or a chicken in wine, but the rest of the time I'm the only one who takes time off from thinking to cook a hamburger. They live on rolls and coffee and sardines."

Mary puts our cups in the sink and then opens a low cupboard. Instead of pots and pans it has stacks of records in it. She pulls out *West Side Story* and then I see there's a record player on a side table. What d'you know? A record player in the kitchen! This Left Bank style of living has its advantages.

"I sit down here and eat and play records while I do my homework," says Mary, which sounds pretty nice.

I ask her if she has any Belafonte, and she says, "Yes, a couple," but she puts on something else. It's slow, but sort of powerful, and it makes you feel kind of powerful yourself, as if you could do anything.

"What's that?" I ask.

"It's called 'The Moldau'—that's a river in Europe. It's by a Czech named Smetana."

I wander around the kitchen and look out the

window. The wind's still howling, but not so hard. I remember the ocean, all gray and powerful, spotted with whitecaps. I'd like to be out on it.

"You know what'd be fun?" I say out loud. "To be out in a boat on the harbor today. If you didn't sink."

"We could take the Staten Island ferry," Mary says.

"Huh?" I hadn't even thought there was really any boat we could get on. "Really? Where do you get it?"

"Down at Sixty-ninth Street and Fourth Avenue. It's quite a ways. I've always gone there in a car. But maybe we could do it on bikes, if we don't freeze."

"We won't freeze. But what about bikes?"

"You can use my brother's. He's away at college. Maybe I can find a windbreaker of his, too." She finds the things and we get ready and go into the living room, where Nina is sitting reading and sipping a glass of wine.

"We're going on our bikes to the ferry and over to Staten Island," Mary says. She doesn't even ask.

"Oh-h-h." It's a long, low note, faintly questioning.

"We thought with the wind blowing and all, it'd be exciting," Mary explains, and I think, Uh-o, that's going to cook it. *My* mother would have kittens if I said I was going out on a ferry in a storm.

But Nina just says, "I see," and goes back to reading her book. I say good-bye and she looks up again and smiles, and that's all.

It's another funny thing—Nina doesn't seem to pay any attention to who Mary brings home, like most mothers are always snooping if their daughter brings home a guy. Without stopping to think, I say, "Do you bring home a lot of guys?"

Mary laughs. "Not a lot. Sometimes one of the boys at school comes home when we're studying for a science test."

I laugh, too, but what I'm thinking of is how Pop would look if I brought a girl home and said we were studying for a test!

14

EXPEDITION BY FERRY

As we ride through Brooklyn the wind belts us around from both sides and right in the teeth. But the sun's beginning to break through, and it's easy riding, no hills.

This part of Brooklyn is mostly rows of houses joined together, or low apartment buildings, with little patches of lawn in front of them. There's lots of trees along the streets. It doesn't look anything like Manhattan, but not anything like the country, either. It's just Brooklyn.

All of a sudden we're circling a golf course.

What d'you know? Right in New York City!

"Ever play golf?" The wind snatches the words out of my mouth and carries them back to Mary. I see her mouth shaping like a "No," but no sound comes my way. I drop back beside her and say, "I'll show you sometime. My pop's got a set of clubs I used a couple of times."

"Probably I better carry the clubs and you play. I can play tennis, though."

We pass the golf course and head down into a sort of main street. Anyway there's lots of banks and dime stores and traffic. Mary leads the way. We make a couple of turns and zigzags and then go under the parkway, and there's the ferry. It's taken us most of an hour to get from Mary's house.

I'm hoping the ferry isn't too expensive, so I'll have plenty of money left for a good lunch. But while I'm mooning, Mary has wheeled her bike right up and paid her own fare. Well, I guess that's one of the things I like about her. She's independent. Still, I'm going to buy lunch.

The ferry is terrific. I'm going to come ride ferries every day it's windy. The boat doesn't roll any, but we stand right up in front and the wind blows clouds of spray in our faces. You can pretend you're on a full-rigged schooner running before a hurricane. But you look down at that choppy gray water, and you know you'd be done if you got blown overboard, even if it is just an old ferryboat in New York harbor.

The ferry ride is fast, only about fifteen minutes. We ride off in Staten Island and start thinking where to go. I know what's first with me.

I ask Mary, "What do you like, hamburgers or sandwiches?"

"Both. I mean either," she says.

The first place we see is a delicatessen, which is about my favorite kind of place to eat anyway. I order a hot pastrami, and Mary says she never had one, but she'll try the same.

"Where could we go on Staten Island?" I say. "I never was here before."

"About the only place I've been is the zoo. I've been there lots of times. The vet let me watch her operate on a snake once."

This is a pretty surprising thing for a girl to tell you in the middle of a mouthful of hot pastrami. The pastrami is great, and they put it on a roll with a lot of olives and onions and relish. Mary likes it too.

"Is the vet a woman? Aren't you scared of snakes?"

"Uh-un, I never was really. But when you're watching an operation, you get so interested you don't think about it being icky or scary. The vet is a woman. She's been there quite a while."

I digest this along with the rest of my sandwich. Then we both have a piece of apple pie. You can tell from the way the crust looks—browned and a little uneven—that they make it right here.

"So shall we go to the zoo?" Mary asks.

"O.K." I get up to get her coat and mine. When I turn around, there she is up by the cashier, getting ready to pay her check.

"Hey, I'm buying lunch," I say, steaming up with the other check.

"Oh, that's all right." She smiles. "I've got it."

I don't care if she's *got* it. I want to *pay* it. I suppose it's a silly thing to get sore about, but it sort of annoys me. Anyway, how do you maneuver around to do something for a girl when she doesn't even know you want to?

The man in the deli gives us directions to get to the zoo, which isn't far. It's a low brick building in a nice park. In the lobby there are some fish tanks, then there's a wing for birds on one side, animals on the other, and snakes straight ahead.

We go for snakes. Mary really seems to like them.

She says, "The vet here likes them, and I guess she got me interested. You know, they don't really understand how a snake moves? Mechanically, I mean. She's trying to find out."

We look at them all, little ones and big ones, and then we go watch the birds. The keeper is just feeding them. The parrot shouts at him, and the pelican and the eagles gobble up their fish and raw meat, but the vulture just sits on his perch looking bored. Probably needs a desert and a dying Legionnaire to whet his appetite.

In the animal wing a strange-looking dame is down at the end, talking to a sleepy tiger.

"Come on, darling, just a little roar. Couldn't you give me just a soft one today?" she's cooing at him. The tiger blinks and looks away.

The lady notices us standing there and says, "He's my baby. I've been coming to see him for fourteen years. Some days he roars for me beautifully."

She has a short conversation with the lion, then moves along with us toward the small cats, a puma and a jaguar. She looks in the next cage, which is empty, and shakes her head mournfully.

"I had the sweetest little leopard. He died last week. Would you believe it? The zoo never let me know he was sick. I could have come and helped take care of him. I might have saved his life."

She goes on talking, sometimes to herself, sometimes to the puma, and we cross over to look at two otters chasing each other up an underwater tunnel.

"What is she, some kind of nut?" Mary says. "Does she think this is her private zoo?"

I shrug. "I suppose she's a little off. But so's my Aunt Kate, the one who gave me Cat. They just happen to like cats better than people. Kate thinks all the stray cats in the world are her children, and I guess this one feels the same way about the big cats here."

We mosey around a little bit more and then head back to the ferry. I make good and sure I'm ahead, and I get to the ticket office and buy two tickets.

"Would you care for a ride across the harbor in my yacht?" I say.

"Why, of course. I'd be delighted," says Mary.

A small thing, but it makes me feel good.

Over in Brooklyn I see a clock on a bank, and it says five o'clock. I do some fast calculating and say, "Uh-oh, I better phone. I'll never make it home by dinnertime."

I phone and get Pop. He's home early from work. Just my luck.

"I got to get this bike back to this kid in Coney," I tell him. "Then I'll be right home. About seven."

"What do you mean *this* bike and *this* kid? Who? Anyway, I thought you were already at Coney Island."

I suppose lawyers just get in the habit of asking questions. I start explaining. "Well, it was awfully cold over in Coney, and we thought we'd go over to Staten Island on the ferry and go to the zoo. So now we just got back to Brooklyn, and I'm downtown and I got to take the bike back."

"So who's 'we'? You got a rat in your pocket?"

I can distract Mom but not Pop. "Well, actually, it's a girl named Mary. It's her brother's bike. He's away in college."

All I can hear now is Pop at the other end of the line, laughing his head off.

"So what's so funny about that?"

"Nothing," he says. "Nothing. Only now I can see what all the shouting was about at breakfast."

"Oh."

"O.K. Now mind you get that girl, as *well* as the bicycle of the brother who goes to college, home safe. Hear? I'll tell your mother you narrowly escaped drowning, and she'll probably save you a bone for dinner. O.K.?"

"O.K. Bye."

Him and his jokes. Ha, ha, ha. Funny, though, him worrying about me getting Mary home safe, when her own mother doesn't worry any.

We start along toward her house slowly, as there's a good deal of traffic now. I'm wondering how to see Mary again without having to ask for her number and phoning and making a date. Something about telephoning I don't like. Besides, I'd probably go out to a pay phone so the family wouldn't listen, and that'd make me feel stupid to begin with.

Just then we start rounding the golf course, and I whack the handle bar of my bike and say, "Hey, that's it!"

"What's it?"

"Golf. Let's play golf. Not now, I don't mean. Next holiday. We've got Election Day coming up. I'll borrow Pop's clubs and take the subway and meet you here. How about ten o'clock?"

"Hunh?" Mary looks startled. "Well, I suppose I could try, or anyway I could walk around."

"It's easy. I'll show you." The two times I played,

I only hit the ball decently about four or five times. But the times I *did* hit it, it seemed easy.

We get to Mary's house and I put the bikes away and give her back her brother's jacket. "I guess I'll go right along. It's getting late. See you Election Day."

"O.K., bye. Say—thanks for the ferry ride!"

15

Wednesday night before Thanksgiving I go down to the delicatessen to buy some Coke, so I can really enjoy myself watching TV. Tom is just finishing work at the flower shop, and I ask him if he wants to come along home.

"Nah. Thanks. I got to be at work early tomorrow." He doesn't sound too cheery.

"How's the job going?"

"O.K., I guess." We walk along a little ways. "The job's not bad, but I don't want to be a florist all my life, and I can't see this job will train me for anything else."

That seems pretty true. It must be tough not getting regular holidays off, too. "You have to work all day tomorrow?" I ask.

"I open the store up at seven and start working on orders we've already got. I'll get through around three or four."

"Hey, you want to come for dinner? We're not eating till evening."

Tom grins. "You cooking the dinner? Maybe you better ask your mother."

"It'll be all right with Mom. Look, I'll ask her and come let you know in the store tomorrow, O.K.?"

"Hmm. Well, sure. Thanks. I've got a date with Hilda later in the evening, but she's got to eat with her folks first."

"O.K. See you tomorrow."

"Right."

Mom says it's all right about Tom coming, so I go down and tell him in the morning. Turns out Mom has asked Kate to have dinner with us, too, which is quite a step. For Kate, I mean. I think she would have turned the invitation down, except no one can bear to hurt Mom's feelings. Kate's been in our house before, of course, but then she just came in to chat or have tea or something. It wasn't like an invitation.

She comes, and she looks like someone from another world. I've never seen her in anything but her old skirts and sneakers, so the "good clothes" she's wearing now must have been hanging in a closet twenty years. The dress and shoes are way out of style, and she's carrying a real old black patent-leather pocketbook. Usually she just lugs her old cloth shopping bag, mostly full of cat goodies. Come to think of it, that's it: Kate lives in a world that is just her own and the cats'. I never saw her trying to fit into the ordinary world before.

Cat knows her right away, though. Clothes don't fool him. He rubs her leg and curls up on the sofa beside her, still keeping a half-open eye on the oven door in the kitchen, where the turkey is roasting.

Tom comes in, also in city clothes—a white shirt and tie and jacket—the first time I ever saw him in them. He sits down on the other side of Cat, who stretches one paw out toward him negligently.

Looking at Kate and Tom sitting there on the sofa, both looking a little ill at ease, I get a funny idea. My family is starting to collect people the way Kate collects homeless cats. Of course, Kate

and Tom aren't homeless. They're people-less—
not part of any family. I think Mom always wanted
more people to take care of, so she's glad to have
them.

Kidding, I ask Kate, "How many cats at your
home for Thanksgiving dinner?"

She stops stroking Cat a minute and thinks.
"Hmm, Susan's got four new kittens, just got their
eyes open. A beautiful little orange one and three
tigers. Then there's two big kittens, strays, and
one old stray tom. Makes eight, that's all. Sometimes I've had lots more than that."

"Doesn't the landlord ever object?" Pop asks.

Kate snorts. "Him! Huh! I pay my rent. And I
have my own padlock on the door, so he can't
come snooping around."

We all sit down to dinner. Pop gives Cat the
turkey neck to crunch up in the kitchen. He finishes that and crouches and stares at us eating.
Kate gives him tidbits, which I'm not supposed to
do. I don't think she really wants to eat the turkey
herself. She's pretty strictly a fruit and yogurt type.

After dinner Tom leaves to meet Hilda, and I
walk home with Kate, carrying a bag of scraps
and giblets for her cats. While she's fiddling with
the two sets of keys to open her door, the man

next door sticks his head out. "Messenger was here a little while ago with a telegram for you. Wouldn't give it to me."

"A telegram?" Kate gapes.

"Yeah. He'll be back." The man looks pleased, like he's been able to deliver some bad news, and pulls his head in and shuts his door.

We go into Kate's apartment, and cats come meowing and rubbing against her legs, and they jump up on the sink and rub and nudge the bag of scraps when she puts it down. Kate is muttering rapidly to herself and fidgeting with her coat and bag and not really paying much attention to the cats, which is odd.

"Lots of people send telegrams on holidays. It's probably just greetings," I say.

"Not to me, they don't!" Kate snaps, also sounding as if they better hadn't.

I go over to play with the little kittens. The marmalade-colored one is the strongest of the litter, and he's learned to climb out of the box. He chases my fingers. Kate finishes feeding the big cats, and she strides over and scoops him back into the box. "You stay in there. You'll get stepped on." She drops Susan back in with her babies to take care of them.

The doorbell rings, and Kate yanks open the door, practically bowling over an ancient little messenger leaning sleepily against the side of the door.

"Take it easy, lady, take it easy. Just sign here," he says.

She signs, hands him the pencil, and slams the door. The orange kitten has got out again, and Kate does come close to stepping on him as she walks across the room tearing open the telegram. He doesn't know enough to dodge feet yet. I scoop him back in this time.

Kate reads the telegram and sits down. She looks quite calm now. She says, "Well, he died."

"Huh? Who?"

"My brother. He's the only person in the world I know who would send me a telegram. So he's dead now."

She repeats it, and I can't figure whether to say I'm sorry or what. I always thought when someone heard of a death in the family, there'd be a lot of crying and commotion. Kate looks perfectly calm, but strange somehow.

"Has he been sick?"

Kate shakes her head. "I don't know. I haven't seen him in twenty years."

There is silence a moment, and then Kate goes on, talking half to herself and half to me. "Mean old coot. He never talked to anyone, except about his money. That's all he cared about. Once he tried to get me to give him money to invest. That's the last time I saw him. He has an old house way up in the Bronx. But we never did get along, even when we were kids."

"Did he have a wife or anything? Who sent the telegram?"

"He's had a housekeeper. Just as mean as him. She'd buy him day-old bread and dented cans of soup because they were cheaper. She suited him fine—saved him money and never talked to him. Well, she'll get his money now, if he left any. That's what she's been waiting for. She sent me the wire."

Twenty years, I think. That's a long time not to be speaking to your own brother, and him living just a ten-cent phone call away. I wonder. She couldn't just not give a hoot about him. They must have been real mad at each other. And mad at the whole world, too. Makes you wonder what kind of parents *they* had, with one of them growing up loving only cats and the other only money.

Kate is staring out the window and stroking an

old stray tomcat between the ears, and it hits me: there isn't a person in the world she loves or even hates. I like cats fine, too, but if I didn't have people that mattered, it wouldn't be so good. I say "So long" quietly and go out.

16

FORTUNE

"I always wondered if the poor soul had any relatives." That's what Mom says when I tell her about Kate's telegram. "And now she's lost her only brother. That's sad."

"I think it's sad she never talked to him for twenty years. All these years I've wished I had a brother," I say.

"If it's her only brother, she's going to have to do something about his estate," says Pop. That legal mind, it never rests. I guess he's got a point about this, though. How is Kate going to deal with lawyers, or undertakers, or anyone? She can't hardly stand to *talk* to people like that.

"What'll she have to do?"

"Maybe I better go see her tomorrow," says Pop. "There can be lots of things—see if he left a will, if he owes any taxes, if he has property that has to be taken care of or sold. You can't tell."

"Kate said he was a miser. Maybe he left her a million. Say, that'd be great!"

"Don't be a dope!" Pop snaps, and he really sounds angry, so I pipe down.

The next morning Pop tells me to go over and see how Kate is. "The way she feels about people, I don't like to just barge in. I'll come by in ten minutes, like I was picking you up to go to a movie or something."

I saunter round the corner onto Third Avenue and stop short. There are two newspaper cars pulled up in front of Kate's building, one red and one black, and a sizable knot of people gathered on the sidewalk. I move in among them.

"That crazy cat lady . . . he musta been a nut too . . . left her about a million . . . a lotta rich cats, how d'ya like that. . . ."

So I guess he did leave her money, and all of a sudden I see it isn't "great." It's going to be trouble. I push through the people and go upstairs without anyone stopping me. When I open Kate's door, old stray tomcat shoots out. He's leaving, and I can see why.

Kate's room is tiny, and it looks like it's filled with a mob. Maybe it's only half a dozen guys, but the photographers are pushing around trying to get shots and the reporters are jabbering.

Orange kitten sticks his head out of the box. Then out he comes, into the sea of feet. I drop him back in and try to get across to Kate. She's pretty well backed into a corner and looking ready to jump out the window. She has her arms folded in front of her, each hand clenching the other elbow, as if to hold herself together. A reporter with a bunch of scratch paper in his hand is crowding her.

"Miss Carmichael"—funny, I never even knew her last name before—"I just want to ask one or two questions. Could you tell us when you last saw your brother?"

"No, I couldn't," she snaps, drawing her head down between her shoulders and trying to melt into the wall.

"Watcha going to do with the money?" a photographer asks. He picks up a cat, one of the big stray kittens, and dumps it on Kate. The cat clings to her and the photographer says, "Hold it now. Just let me snap a picture."

He takes two steps back.

At the first step the room is silent. At the second step a shattering caterwaul goes up. He has stepped on the adventurous orange kitten.

The scream freezes us all, except Kate. She shoots out of her corner, knowing instantly what has happened. The kitten is jerking slightly now, and bright, bright blood is coming out of its mouth. With one violent, merciful stroke Kate finishes it. She picks the limp body up and wraps it neatly in a paper towel and places it in the wastebasket.

The room is still silent for one congealed instant. Kate seems almost to have forgotten the crowd of men. Then two of them make hastily for the door. The photographer shuffles his feet and says, "Gee, m'am, I didn't mean . . . I wouldn't for the world . . ."

Kate whirls and screams at him: "Get out! Get out, all of you! Leave me and my cats alone! I never asked you in here!"

At that moment my pop comes in the door. Of course he doesn't know anything about the kitten, but he takes in the general situation and herds the two remaining newspapermen to the door. He gives them his card and home address and tells them to look him up a little later.

My knees suddenly feel weak and I slump onto the sofa, and my eyes swivel round to the little package in the wastebasket. It would be the strongest one. I really never saw anything get killed right in front of me before. It hits you.

Pop is trying to calm Kate down. She's facing him, grabbing each sleeve of his coat. "What am I going to do? What can I do? I don't want his money. I don't want anything from anyone. I just want to be let alone!"

"Take it easy, Kate, take it easy. You don't have to let anyone into your apartment. About the inheritance, well, I'll have to look into that." Over his shoulder Pop signals to me to go home and get Mom.

I go home and explain the situation to Mom, and she comes back with me. One photographer and a couple of reporters are still hanging around, and the guy snaps a picture of me and Mom at the door. Mom scoots on up. Bad as I feel, I still get a charge out of getting my picture taken for a paper.

"Hey, kid," one of the reporters shoves in front of me, "about this Miss Carmichael. Does she act pretty strange, like talking to herself on the street and stuff?"

I see the story he's trying to build up. While it's true in a way, if you really know Kate it's not. Anyway, I'm against it. I say, "Nah. She's all right. She's just sort of scared of people, and she likes cats."

"How many cats she got?"

There have been up to a dozen on a busy day, but again I play it down. "She's got a mother cat with kittens. Sometimes a stray or two. Don't get sucked in by all that jazz these dumb kids around here'll give you."

"She gets all that money, you think she'll buy a big house, set up a home for stray cats?"

I shrug. "I don't know. She doesn't want the money anyway. She just wants to be let alone."

"Doesn't want the money!" the photographer chips in. "Boy, she must be *really* nuts! I'm going back to the office."

The reporter says he's going to wait and talk to my pop, and I go on upstairs to see what's doing.

Kate is sitting on the sofa, sniffling and wiping her eyes and muttering, but looking calmer. Mom is making tea. Pop is looking out the window, scratching his head.

Kate gulps and draws a big breath. "Tell them I don't want his old money. Tell them to give it to someone else. Tell them to leave me alone. I just want my own place and my cats. They can't make me move, can they? I've lived here thirty years. I couldn't go anyplace else."

She gulps and sniffs some more, and Mom brings her a cup of tea. The stray kittens jump up to see if it's anything good and nuzzle into her lap. Kate takes a sip of tea and asks Pop again, "They can't make me move, can they?" This seems to be what worries her most.

"No-o," says Pop, "it's only . . ."

He's interrupted by a knock on the door, and I go open it a crack. A guy says he's the landlord. As soon as Kate hears his voice, she yelps at him, "I paid my rent, first of the month like always. Don't you come bothering me!"

"It's about the cats," he says. "People outside saying you got a dozen cats in here. There's a law, you know."

He's a seedy-looking, whining kind of a man, and he looks real pleased with himself when he says there's a law about cats.

Kate jumps right at him. "I'm not breaking any laws. I know you. You just want to get me out of here and rent the place for more money. You leave me alone!"

The man whines, "There's a law, that's all. I don't want no violation slapped on my building."

Pop comes over and tells the man there's just a mother cat with kittens. "There's a couple of strays here, too, right now, but I'll take them home with me."

"There's a law, that's all. Also, I got a right to inspect the premises." Pop shows no signs of letting him in, and he shuffles and grumbles and goes away.

"Lock the door," Kate snaps. "I keep it locked all the time."

Pop says he's going home to make some phone calls and try to figure out what's going on. He takes down the name and address of Kate's brother and asks her if she's sure there are no other relatives. She says she never heard of any. Pop goes, and Kate insists that I lock the door after him.

She gets up and starts stirring around getting food out for the cats. She buys fish and chicken livers for them, even though she hardly eats any meat herself. She listens at the back door a moment to make sure no one's out there, then opens the door and puts out the garbage and wastebasket. There goes the adventurous kitten. You got to hand it to Kate. She has no sniffling sentimentality about her cats. Kitten's dead, it's dead, that's all. She doesn't mope over the limp mite of fur. In fact, anything to do with cats she's got sense and guts. They're her family. I don't know that I could have put that kitten out of its misery.

Just as long as the world doesn't throw any stray fortunes at her, Kate does fine. But when people get in her way, she needs someone like Pop.

Mom says she'll stick around a while and tells me to take the two stray kittens home, just in case the landlord comes back trying to make trouble.

"O.K., great—Cat'll have some company!"

Kate sniffs. "He'll hate it. Cats don't like other cats pushing into their house."

She's right, of course. I put the kittens down at home, and Cat hisses at them and then runs them under the radiator in the kitchen. Then he sits down in the doorway and glowers at them, on guard.

Things simmer down gradually. Mom and I and

sometimes Tom, who's right at the flower shop on the corner, take turns checking on Kate and doing shopping for her, or going with her so she doesn't get badgered by people. But pretty soon everyone in the neighborhood forgets all about her and her inheritance. They see her buying just the same old cat food and cottage cheese and fruit, and they probably figure the whole thing was a phony.

It wasn't though. Pop finds out her brother did leave a will. He lined up his funeral, left something to his housekeeper, something to a little restaurant owner way downtown—apparently that was his one big luxury, a decent meal twice a year when he went down to buy more stocks—and the rest to Kate.

Pop says it may take months or years to clear up the estate, but he says Kate can get her share all put in trust for her with some bank, and they'll take care of all the legalities and taxes and just pay her as much or little as she wants out of the income. And she can leave the whole kit and caboodle to a cat home in her will if she wants to, which will probably make her tightwad brother spin in his grave. I asked her once, and she said maybe she'd leave some to the Children's Aid, because there are a lot of stray children in New York City that need looking after, as well as cats. She's getting to think about people some.

17
TELEPHONE NUMBERS

There are some disadvantages to not getting a girl's phone number. This sort of date I had with Mary for golf on Election Day fell through. In the first place, I was sick in bed with the flu, and Mom wouldn't have let me out for anything, and secondly, it was pouring rain. Without the phone number, there wasn't any way I could let her know, and I didn't even know a street address to write to later.

By the time I got finished with the flu, we were into Thanksgiving and then all the trouble with

Kate. Time passed and I felt rottener about standing her up without a word, and I couldn't get up my nerve to go out to Coney and just appear on her doorstep. I could have found the house all right, once I was out there.

The first week of Christmas vacation the phone rings late one afternoon and Pop answers it. He says, "Just one minute, please," and I know right away from his voice it isn't someone he knows.

"Young lady on the phone for you, Dave," he says, and he enjoys watching me gulp.

"Hullo?" a rather tight, flat little voice asks. "Is this Dave—uh, Mitchell—uh, I mean, with Cat?"

I recognize it's Mary, all right, even if she does sound strange and scared.

"Oh, hi!" I say. "Sure, it's me! I'm awfully sorry about that day we were going to play golf. I was in bed with the flu, and then I didn't know your phone number or . . ."

"Oh, that's all right," she says. "I wondered what happened."

There's a slight pause, and I see Pop grinning and pretending to read his paper. I turn around so I won't see him.

"Where are you now, out in Coney?" I ask Mary.

"No, as a matter of fact, I'm in Macy's." Her

voice trails off a little, but then she starts in again. "As a matter of fact, that's why I called. You see, I was supposed to meet Mom here at five, and she hasn't come, and I bought all these Christmas presents, and I forgot about the tax or something, and this is my last dime."

She stops. I see now why she sounds scared, and I get a curdled feeling in my stomach, too, because what if the dime runs out in the phone and she's cut off? I'll never find her in Macy's. It's too big.

"Pop!" I yelp. "There's this girl I know is in a phone booth in Macy's and her dime is going to run out and she hasn't anymore money. What'll I do?"

"Get the phone number of the booth and call her back. Here—" He gives me a pencil.

What a relief. Funny I never thought of that. You just somehow don't think of a phone booth having a number.

Mary sounds pretty relieved, too. I get the number and call her back, and with Pop making suggestions here and there we settle that I'll go over to Macy's and meet her on the ground floor near Thirty-fourth Street and Broadway at the counter where they're selling umbrellas for $2.89, which Mary says she can see from the phone booth.

"O.K." I say, and then I sort of don't want to hang up. It's fun talking. So I go on. "Look, just in case we miss each other at Macy's, what's your phone number at home, so I could call you sometime?"

"COney 7-1218."

"O.K. Well, good-bye. I'll be right over. To Macy's, I mean."

I grab my coat and check to see if I've got money. Pop asks if I'm going to bring her home for dinner.

"Gee, I don't know." I hadn't given a thought to what we'd do. "I guess so, maybe, if her mother hasn't come by then. I'll call you if we do anything else."

"O.K.," Pop says.

I go out and hustle through the evening rush-hour crowds to the subway. The stores are all open evenings now, for Christmas, so the crowds are going both ways.

I get to the right corner of Macy's, and I see Mary right away. Everyone else is rushing about and muttering to themselves, and she's standing there looking lost. In fact she looks so much like a waif that the first thing I say is, "Hi! Shall we go get something to eat?"

"Yes, I'm starved. I was just going to get a doughnut when I found I'd run out of money."

"Let's go home and you can have dinner with us then. But what about your mother? Won't she be looking for you?"

Mary shifts her feet and looks tired. "I don't know. Probably if she came and I wasn't here, she'd figure I'd gone home."

I try to think a minute, which is hard to do with all these people shoving around you. Mary starts to pick up her two enormous shopping bags, and I take them from her, still trying to think. At the subway entrance I see the phone booth.

"That's the thing," I say. "Why don't you call your house and see if your mother left a message or something?"

"Well . . ." Mary stands by the phone looking confused and in fact about ready to cry. I suddenly decide the best thing we can do is get home and sit down where it's quiet. Waiting fifteen minutes or so to phone can't make much difference.

We get home pretty fast and I introduce Mary to Mom and Pop. She sinks into the nearest chair and takes off her shoes.

"Excuse me," she says. "I just bought these heels, and it's awful wearing them!"

She wiggles her toes and begins to look better. Mom offers her a pair of slippers and Pop passes some potato chips.

Mom says, "Poor child, did you try to do all your Christmas shopping at once?"

"Well, actually, I was having fun just looking for a long while. I have two little cousins that I don't really have to get much for, but I love looking at all the toys. I spent quite a while there. Then I did the rest of my shopping in a rush, and everything is so crowded, and I got mixed up on my money or the sales tax and only had a dime left, and I missed my mother or she forgot."

She stretches out her toes to touch Cat, who is sitting in front of her. "I couldn't think what to do. It's so hard to think when your feet hurt."

"It certainly is," agrees Mom. She goes out to the kitchen to finish fixing dinner, and Pop suggests Mary better phone her home. She gets her father, and her mother has left a message that she was delayed and figured Mary would go home alone. Mary gives her father our address and tells him she'll be home by nine.

We must have hit a lucky day because we have a real good dinner: slices of good whole meat, not mushed up stuff, and potatoes cooked with cheese in them, and salad, and a lemon meringue pie from the bakery, even.

After dinner we sit around a little while, and Pop says I better take Mary home, and he gives me money for a cab at the end of the subway. When Mary gives the driver her home address, I say it over to myself a few times so I'll remember.

Suddenly I wonder about something. "Say, how'd you know *my* phone number?"

"I looked it up," she says simply. "There's about twenty-eleven Mitchells in the Manhattan phone book, but only one in the East Twenties, so I figured that must be you."

"Gee, that's true. You must have had an awful time, though, standing in the phone booth with your feet hurting, going through all those Mitchells."

Says Mary, "Oh, no. I did it one rainy afternoon at home, weeks ago."

Well, what do you know.

The two stray kittens gradually make themselves at home. Somehow or other Cat has taught them that he's in charge here, and he just chases them for fun now and again, when he's not busy sleeping.

As for keeping cats in my room, that's pretty well forgotten. For one thing, Mom really likes them. She sneaks the kittens saucers of cream and bits of real hamburger when no one's looking, and she likes talking to them in the kitchen. She doesn't pick them up, but just having them in the room sure doesn't give her asthma.

IT'S LIKE THIS, CAT

The only time we have any trouble from the cats is one evening when Pop comes home and the two kittens skid down the hall between his legs, with Cat after them. He scales his hat at the lot of them and roars down the hall to me, "Hey, Davey! When are you getting rid of these cats? I'm not fixing to start an annex to Kate's cat home!"

"I'm sure Davey will find homes for them," Mom says soothingly, but getting a little short of breath, the way she does any time she's afraid one of us is losing his temper.

In fact, one thing this cat business seems to have established is that me and Pop fighting is the main cause of Mom's asthma. So we both try to do a little better, and a lot of things we used to argue and fight about, like my jazz records, we just kid each other about now. But now and then we still work up to a real hassle.

I've been taking a history course the first semester at school. It's a real lemon—just a lot of preaching about government and citizenship. The second semester I switch to a music course. This is O.K. with the school—but not with Pop. Right away when I bring home my new program, he says, "How come you're taking one less course this half?"

I explain that I'm taking music, and also biology, algebra, English, and French.

"Music!" he snorts. "That's recreation, not a course. Do it on your own time!"

"Pop, it's a course. You think the school signs me up for an hour of home record playing?"

"They might," he grunts. "You're not going to loaf your way through school if I have anything to say about it."

"Loaf!" I yelp. "Four major academic subjects is more than lots of the guys take."

Mom comes and suggests that Pop better go over to school with me and talk it over at the school office. He does, and for once I win a round—I keep music for this semester. But he makes sure that next year I'm signed up all year for five majors: English, French, math, chemistry, and European history. I'll be lucky if I have time to breathe.

I go down to the flower shop to grouse to Tom. It's after Valentine's Day, and business is slack and the boss is out.

"Why does Pop have to come butting into my business at school? Doesn't he even think the school knows what it's doing?"

"Aw, heck," says Tom, "your father's the one

has to see you get into college or get a job. Some-times schools do let kids take a lot of soft courses, and then they're out on a limb later."

"Huh. He just likes to boss everything I do."

"So—he cares."

"Huh." I'm not very ready to buy this, but then I remember Tom's father, who *doesn't* care. It makes me think.

"Besides," says Tom, "half the reason you and your father are always bickering is that you're so much alike."

"Me? Like *him*?"

"Sure. You're both impatient and curious, got to poke into everything. As long as there's a bone on the floor, the two of you worry it."

Mr. Palumbo comes back to the shop then, and Tom gets busy with the plants. I go home, wondering if I really am at all like Pop. I never thought of it before.

It's funny about fights. Pop and I can go along real smooth and easy for a while, and I think: Well, he really isn't a bad guy, and I'm growing up, we can see eye to eye—all that stuff. Then, whoosh! I hardly know what starts it, but a fight boils up, and we're both breathing fire like drag-ons on the loose.

We get a holiday Washington's birthday, which
is good because there's a TV program on Tuesday,
the night before the holiday, that I hardly ever get
to watch. It's called *Out Beyond,* and the people
in it are very real, not just good guys and bad
guys. There's always one character moving
around, keeping you on the edge of your chair,
and by the time it all winds up in a surprise end-
ing, you find this character is not a real person,
he's supernatural. The program goes on till
eleven o'clock, and Mom won't let me watch it on
school nights.

I get the pillows comfortably arranged on the
floor, with a big bottle of soda and a bag of popcorn within easy reach. The story starts off with
some nature shots of a farm and mountains in the
background and this little kid playing with his
grandfather. There's a lot of people in it, but gradually you get more and more suspicious of dear
old grandpa. He's taking the kid for a walk when
a thunderstorm blows up.

Right then, of course, we have to have the alter-
nate sponsor. He signs off, finally, and up comes
Pop.

"Here, Davey old boy, we can do better than
that tonight. The Governor and the Mayor are on

a TV debate about New York City school reorganization."

At first I figure he's kidding, so I just growl, "Who cares?" He switches the channel.

I jump up, tipping over the bottle of soda on the way. "Pop, that's not fair! I'm right in the middle of a program, and I been waiting weeks to watch it because Mom won't let me on school nights!"

Pop goes right on tuning his channel. "Do you good to listen to a real program for a change. There'll be another western on tomorrow night."

That's the last straw. I shout, "See? You don't even know what you're talking about! It's not a western."

Pop looks at me prissily. "You're getting altogether too upset about these programs. Stop it and behave yourself. Go get a sponge to mop up the soda."

"It's your fault! Mop it up yourself!" I'm too mad now to care what I say. I charge down the hall to my room and slam the door.

I hear the TV going for a few minutes, then Pop turns it off and goes in the kitchen to talk to Mom. In a little while he comes down and knocks on my door. Knocks—that's something. Usually he just barges in.

"Look here now, Dave, we've got to straighten a few things out quietly. Your mother says she told you you could watch that program, whatever it was. So O.K., go ahead, you can finish it."

"Yeah, it's about over by now." I'm still sore, and besides Pop's still standing in my door, so I figure there's a hitch in this somewhere.

"But anyway, you shouldn't get so sore about an old television program that you shout 'Mop it up yourself' at me."

"Hmm."

"Hmm, nothing."

"Well, I don't think you should turn a guy's TV program off in the middle without even finding out about it."

Pop says "Hmm" this time, and we both stand and simmer down.

I look at my watch. It's a quarter to eleven. I say, "Well, O.K. I might as well see the end. Sorry I got sore."

Pop moves out of the doorway. He says, "Hereafter I will only turn off your TV programs before they start, not in the middle."

Just as I get the TV on and settle down, the doorbell rings.

"Goodness, who could that be so late?" says Mom.

Pop goes to the door. It's Tom, and Hilda is with him. I turn off the television set—I've lost track of what's happening, and it doesn't seem to be the grandfather who's the spook after all. It's the first time Hilda has been to our house, and Tom introduces her around. Then there's one of those moments of complete silence, with everyone looking embarrassed, before we all start to speak at once.

"Hilda came to the beach with us," I say.

"I told Tom we shouldn't come so late," says Hilda.

Pop says, "Not late at all. Come in and sit down."

Hilda sits on the sofa, where Cat is curled up. He looks at her, puts his head back and goes on sleeping.

Mom brings coffee and cookies in from the kitchen, and I pour the rest of the popcorn into a bowl and pass it around. Tom stirs his coffee vigorously and takes one sip and puts the cup down.

"Reason we came so late," he says, "Hilda and I have been talking all evening. We want to get married."

Pop doesn't look as surprised as I do. "Congratulations!" he says.

Tom says, "Thanks" and looks at Hilda, and she blushes. Really. Tom drinks a little more coffee and then he goes on: "The trouble is, I can't get married on this flower-shop job."

"Doesn't pay enough?" Pop asks.

"Well, it's not just the pay. The job isn't getting me anywhere I want to go. So that's what we've been talking about all evening. Finally we went up to Times Square and talked to the guys in the Army and Navy and Air Force recruiting office. You know, I'd get drafted in a year or two, anyway. I've decided to enlist in the Army."

"Goodness, you may get sent way out West for years and years!" says Mom.

"No, not if I enlist in the Army. That's for three years. But I can choose what specialist school I want to go into, and there's this Air Defense Command—it's something to do with missiles. In that I can also choose what metropolitan area I want to be stationed in. I can choose New York, and we could get married, and I might even be able to go on taking college courses at night school, with the Army paying for most of it."

Pop says, "You sound like the recruiting officer himself. You sure of all this?"

"I'll have to check some more," says Tom. "The

recruiting officer, as a matter of fact, tried to persuade me to shoot for officers' training and go into the Army as a career. But then I would be sent all over, and anyway, I don't think Army life would be any good for Hilda."

"I can see you have put in a busy evening," says Pop. "Well, shove back the coffee cups, and I'll break out that bottle of champagne that's been sitting in the icebox since Christmas."

I go and retrieve my spilled bottle of soda. There's still enough left for one big glass. Pop brings out the champagne, and the cork blows and hits the ceiling. Cat jumps off the sofa and stands, half crouched and tail twitching, ready to take cover.

Pop fills little glasses for them and raises his to Tom and Hilda. "Here's to you—a long, happy life!"

We drink, and then I raise my glass of soda. "Here's to Cat! Tom wouldn't even be standing here if it wasn't for Cat."

That's true, and we all drink to Cat. He sits down and licks his right front paw.